The Fall of Eden

Michael Dann

To my wife Kellie

Thank you for your unwavering
support and for allowing me to
chase my dream in the creation of
this novel.
Without you and your belief in
me, none of this would have been
possible.

Chapter 1

Michael

Thunder echoes through the night sky as rain begins to trickle down. Everyone runs for cover except one man in the middle of the sidewalk. He lowers the hood from his jacket allowing his face to embrace the heavenly water. He closes his eyes and it comforts him, bringing him a moment of peace before he heads for a nearby church. As he enters he blesses himself and looks around. No one is in sight, but he knows where to go. He makes his way to the empty confession booths and takes a seat within. He doesn't have to wait long before he hears someone moving behind the divider.

"Forgive me, Father, for I have sinned," says the man.

The priest opens the sliding door over the screen of the confessional booth ready to communicate with the man, but before he can do so he is interrupted.

"It has been—" He pauses and scratches his head to contemplate, "—a month since my last confession. And it will be my last."

"What has brought this on, my child?" the priest asks, but he is met with a long and uncomfortable silence. The priest coughs to clear his throat and shifts in his seat before trying again. "May I ask what has brought this on?"

"I'm sorry," the stranger responds, sniffing,, "I...I have lost faith in Him. Don't get me wrong: I believe in Him, but I do not care for Him."

The priest hears more sniffing and a deep sigh from the confessor. "I don't understand, my son."

"I have buried nearly every single family member I have. Mum and Dad, my brothers, all gone—well, except one."

"I know life may seem hard at times and it may seem even harder to see his plan for us—" the priest begins, but is cut off abruptly by the stranger.

"SO, HIS PLAN IS TO KILL ME!" he yells at the priest through the screen, his voice echoing throughout the empty church.

The priest is at a loss for words and takes his time to respond. "You...you are ill?" he asks.

"Cancer," the man responds after some time.

The priest is saddened by this. He lets out a sigh and rests his head in his hands. "I will pray for you—"

"Save your prayers, Father. I'm done with your Lord," the man says hastily before he exits the booth.

The priest quickly chases after him but all that he sees is the stranger exiting the church. The priest raises his hands to the heavens and prays out loud, "Father, watch over him during his darkest hours." He then makes the sign of the cross and hopes that his prayer was heard before whispering to himself, "He's going to need your guidance."

In deep thought, the man walks back to his car. Unfazed by the darkness of the night, he ventures through it like it is his friend. He enters a car park with only one car still occupying a space and looks around. He sees the dark empty oval of the vacant children's playground before approaching his car. He sighs and unlocks his vehicle with a beep, then closing his eyes he pauses for a moment before he gets in, starts the ignition and stares at himself in the rear-view mirror. He gives his distracted head a shake to try and refocus his mind, then he buckles his seatbelt and exhales once again.

He drives off, turning at a nearby street and arriving at a house only a few streets away from the church. He reaches for a controller in the centre console of his car, activates the garage door and parks his car in a sombre mood. This quickly changes when he hears children's laughter coming from inside the house.

A smile spreads across his face. "Come on," he whispers, trying to encourage himself.

He closes the garage and listens one last time to the nothingness before slowly reaching for the door handle and entering the mudroom of his house where he is instantly bombarded by noise. While taking off his wet shoes, he looks up and smiles, admiring his wife in front of the stove cooking a family dinner. Suddenly, his troubles melt away as she walks over and greets him with a kiss.

"Hey, babe!"

"Hey, gorgeous."

"How was your day?" she asks as she heads back over to the stove to check on the dinner.

He feels a little teary, so he gives a default answer as he hangs up his work bag on one of the hooks within the mudroom.

"Yeah, work was good. I got everything done earlier than I thought so I left," he responds before entering the kitchen where two little boys excited to see their father run over to greet him with hugs.

"Dad!" they cry in unison.

Hudson, the eight-year-old, throws his arms around him and squeezes as hard as he can. Four-year-old Isaiah slowly makes his way to his Dad. He does not make eye contact, distracted by the tablet in his hand. He then leans into his Dad's legs expecting him to make the effort of hugging him. His father obliges and leans down to give him a hug. Isaiah then walks back to the lounge, still with his head buried in his tablet.

"Michael!" Kelly calls, a little agitated. "You finished work early and only now you're coming home?"

Michael is a little taken back by his wife's tone.

"I really could've used some help with the kids today, if you finished early."

"Sorry, I had to see a friend."

"Who?"

"Just a work friend," Michael quickly responds, caught off guard, "but he wasn't home, so it was a waste of time."

Kelly looks at him. "Hmm. Okay, well, dinner will be ready in five."

"I'm going to take a shower," Michael announces, relieved she's dropped the issue as he walks to their room. As he preps himself to head into the shower he begins to dwell on the doctor's appointment he had earlier that day and what the priest had told him. He is jolted from his thoughts when he hears someone knocking on the bathroom door.

"Yes?" he calls.

"Is everything okay?" Kelly asks in a worried tone. "The doors locked."

"All good. I'm hopping out now," he quickly says as he washes some soap over himself.

"Good, 'cos you have been in there for nearly ages."

Michael is shocked at how long he has been in the shower; he can't even remember getting in

"I'll be waiting at the dinner table for you," Kelly tells him.

"Okay," Michael finally responds.

He makes his way to the table to find his wife waiting for him and notices she hasn't touched her meal and her arms are folded. He cautiously takes his seat whilst still looking at his wife, then they both reach for their cutlery.

"You took so long that the kids have already eaten," Kelly tells him as she begins to cut up her steak.

"Oh…okay," he replies, adjusting his glasses on his face.

Kelly slowly chews her food and adjusts her own glasses to get a better view of her silent husband. "How did the scans and blood test go today?"

Alarmed, Michael's eyes dart back to his wife.

"Did you think I'd forget?" she asks as she places her cutlery beside her dinner plate.

Michael begins to replay the doctor's words over in his head. He starts to get emotional, and his eyes begin to well up.

Noticing this, Kelly reaches for his hands to comfort him and says reassuringly, "Hey, it's going to be okay. We'll get through this together."

His mouth opens but no words are spoken, then he slowly gains the confidence to speak. "Doctor says—"

Kelly grips his hands tighter.

"—I have prostate cancer."

Kelly sinks back into her chair, expressionless and pale.

"Kel!" She doesn't reply, so Michael tries again. "Kel…are you okay"?

Finally her eyes have movement in them. They glance over at her husband. She has no encouraging words for him, so Michael tries to be brave.

"Don't worry we'll get through this. I'll make it through this," he says calmly, trying to reassure his wife.

A tear trickles from one of Kelly's eyes. She quickly wipes it away trying to hide it from her husband and musters enough strength to give him a broken smile.

"I know we will, hun," she replies, gripping Michael's hands even tighter than before.

They finish their dinner and, side by side, clean up the table and stack the dishwasher.

"Did you want to put the boys to bed and say goodnight to Emma?" Kelly asks Michael exhaustedly. "I need a shower."

"Yeah, okay," Michael replies as he heads into the lounge while his wife makes her way to their bedroom.

Michael checks in the lounge, but Hudson and Isaiah are not there. "Boys?"

He makes his way to their bedroom and as he walks down the corridor he can already hear one of the boy's tablets blaring. He enters their room and notices they are both already fast asleep in bed; Hudson's tablet was next to him still on, but Isaiah's tablet was flat on his face, turned off due to a flat battery. Michael couldn't hold back his fatherly smile as he gathered both of their tablets. He makes sure his sons are both under their blankets and tucks them in for the night. He then turns on their night light and switches off the room light.

"I love you both, my two little men," he says before leaving their room.

After putting their tablets on charge Michael checks in on Emma, his fifteen-year-old daughter, who is still studying in her room.

"Hey, don't study too much. Me and mum are going to bed."

"I won't, I'm finishing up soon," Emma replies from her study desk.

"Okay, well night, night," Michael says as he closes her door.

"Goodnight," Emma responds.

Michael arrives in the master bedroom to find Kelly is already in bed applying moisturiser to her hands and face.

"How are the kids?" she asks.

"Yeah, the boys were already in their beds asleep."

Kelly's jaw drops in shock. "Really?"

"Yeah, must have been a busy day at school. Emma's still studying, but she said she's going to bed shortly."

Kelly finishes moisturising, readjusts the blanket and takes a deep breath."So… do you want to talk about your doctor's appointment?"

A heavy silence fills the air between them.

"Maybe another time," Michael replies as he sits on his side of the bed. "I just want a good night's sleep."

"Oh, okay. You must be exhausted after the day you've had."

Kelly leans in for a goodnight kiss.

"I promise I will talk about it, just not tonight," Michael reassures her.

"That's okay, don't stress," Kelly reassures him as she rolls over to her side of the bed.

Now alone with his thoughts, Michael stares up at the ceiling, his mind racing. He knows his life is about to change and he is now in uncharted waters. This is something that scares him greatly, not knowing what is ahead of him or what could potentially happen. On the other side of the bed, Kelly hops out and begins to walk towards the toilet.

"You still awake?" she asks as her eyes adjust to the dark.

Michael finds this comment odd; hadn't they only just switched off the light? "It's only been like five minutes babe, gimme a chance."

"Babe, look at your phone. It's almost half one."

"What!" Michael cries, reaching for his phone. He is shocked to see that yet again he has lost track of time.

"That can't be!" he says out loud as he sits up in bed and places his phone back on his bedside table.

Kelly sits beside him and rubs his arm and shoulder. "Are you sure you're alright?"

Still confused, Michael sighs. Kelly continues to rub her husband's arms for comfort.

Finally, Michael finds the courage to speak.

"I…don't want to die." Finally this realisation comes crashing down on him.

Kelly catches his drooping head into her lap and he gently cries.

Kelly feels a sense of duty building up inside of her. She needs to comfort her fragile husband in his moment of need.

"We're going to get through this, together," she says as she caresses his head. "All the years I have known you, I have never seen you quit once."

Michael regains his composure as he looks into his wife's reassuring eyes. He nods his head delicately as he lies back down and Kelly covers him with the blanket.

"Get some sleep and we'll talk more in the morning."

Kelly waits until she can hear the steady deeper breaths of sleep from Michael before she gets back up and goes into the bathroom. She locks the door, checking first that he is asleep, and only then does she allow herself to cry.

Chapter 2

Friend or Foe

Morning breaks through the curtain, shining a ray of warmth onto Michael's face and peacefully waking him. He looks over and sees that Kelly has already made her side of the bed. He pauses at first then pounces out of bed when he smells breakfast seeping through the bedroom door. He makes his way to the dining room, throwing on his shirt and is greeted by his two boys who seem to be glued to their tablets again at the breakfast table.

"Morning Dad!" they say, barely raising their eyes.

"Good morning, boys," he replies, smiling at them both, then he looks over at his daughter. She is sitting at the furthest side of the breakfast table, not wanting to be disturbed by her brothers. "Good morning, Emma."

"Hmm," is all Michael hears from her.

He joins them at the table with a bit of pep in his step, as if he has forgotten about his condition already.

"Mum said you had a rough night last night, so we let

you sleep in," Hudson tells him politely.

Annoyed, Kelly looks over at Hudson trying to warn him not to say anything further on the matter.

"What?" Hudson asks, shrugging his shoulders at his mother before finishing off his breakfast.

"It's ok, Bub," Michael comforts Hudson.

"Oh Dad, it's the first of December!" Hudson cries with excitement as he stands up. "Can we put up our Christmas lights and Christmas tree tonight?"

Michael teases his son by taking a moment to think about it.

"I suppose we could," he says as he smiles cheekily at his son.

"YES!" Hudson responds.

Hearing his brother getting excited, Isaiah pauses his tablet and taps his big brother on the shoulder. "What? What's happening?"

"It is almost Christmas, so tonight Dad is going to help us put up the Christmas tree and lights," Hudson explains to Isaiah.

"Yay!" Isaiah responds as he jumps up and down, then they both hug their father.

"Now you're going to HAVE to keep your promise, you know that right?" Kelly warns her husband as she hands him his breakfast. "Getting them both all excited like that."

"I know, but I keep my promises," he smiles back at his wife.

The peace that settles over the breakfast table is suddenly ruined by a news report on the TV blaring in the lounge.

"Another casualty has died due to gang violence in the streets. A young boy has caught a ricocheted bul..." Kelly quickly changes the TV channel before the news reporter could finish her sentence.

"Over a year has passed since China's attack on America," another news reporter says as the screen shows women and children fleeing for their lives.

Kelly turns the TV off altogether. Michael and Kelly look at one another with concern, then she places the remote control down on a nearby table.

"What happened?" Hudson asks inquisitively.

"Nothing Hudson…the TV was too loud, so I turned it off," Kelly answers quickly while Michael gives her a nod.

"I'm glad we live in Australia!" Emma says out loud as she eats her breakfast.

Shortly afterwards, while Michael is looking frantically for his work bag, Kelly tells her husband, "It's getting worse every year. Why is it always in the lead up to Christmas?"

Michael is only partially listening as he gets himself ready to go to work, but he tells Kelly flippantly, "It's the Devil's month."

"Huh?"

Michael finds some socks and starts to put them on. Kelly places her hands on top of his to get him to stop what he is doing and focus.

"What do you mean, 'The Devil's month'?"

"Well, at work I've heard people calling this month the Devil's month," he explains as Kelly moves her hands and he continues putting on his socks and sprays himself with deodorant. "They say it's a godless month, with a lot of death and chaos occurs arounds this time."

"That is the stupidest thing I've ever heard!" Kelly exclaims, screwing her face up in disgust as they both leave the bedroom. "I hope you don't believe in this so-called stupid season."

"Of course not. I don't have any beliefs anymore," Michael replies, turning towards his wife with a smug look.

"Right, and what's this then?" Kelly points to a tattoo of a Rosary wrapped around Michael's arm and shoulder.

"That is out of respect for my grandmothers. You know they're both true believers." He picks up his work polo shirt which is hanging from one of the dining chairs and slips it on.

"Well, why did you get that tattoo blessed then, huh?"

"It's a superstition thing. When I was younger, I felt I played better football knowing my shoulder was blessed," Michael retorts, then he poses in his workwear and asks Kelly, "Okay, how do I look?"

"Oh, hell no! You aren't going to work today!" Kelly argues.

"That's blasphemy," Michael smirks at his wife as he makes his way to the mudroom to find his work bag.

"I'm not Catholic, Michael, so I can say whatever I want," Kelly teases, then her tone changes as she crosses her arms. "But seriously, why are you going to work? We should be talking about what our next steps are."

Michael pauses for a moment, then he puts down his bag and approaches her.

"I promise I'm fine. We can talk about this when I get

home." He picks up his bag, then he goes back to comfort Kelly by kissing her.

"Love you," he says softly.

"Love you too," Kelly sighs, her expression one of defeat as she watches him go.

Michael gets into his car and opens the garage, then as soon as he reverses the vehicle and starts to drive his mind begins to wander again. Only this time he thinks about his family and what life would be like without him in the picture. He starts to tear up as he imagines his children all grown up. He wonders how tall they'll grow and what features they'll inherit from him; who will teach the boys how to shave and what type of career path will Emma choose? Panic begins to set in. There's a lot to think about, especially now knowing his life has a time limit.

A car horn close by breaks the reverie.

Startled, Michael jumps in fright and blinks rapidly. He begins to breathe intensely as he tries to find his bearings. He looks around and finds he's already parked at the train station, but has missed his train. Annoyed, he gets out of the car and makes his way to the platform ready to catch the next one. As he waits, he shakes his head and wonders to himself, *what's going on with me?* He squints and looks around. Only two other people are on the same platform, unaware that Michael is having a mini breakdown. *Get it together!* he scolds himself. He closes his eyes and takes in a deep breath before breathing out gently, then he hears the horn of the next train.

As the train makes its stop, Michael enters the carriage but does not sit just yet. Instead, he makes his way towards the end carriage, wanting to be left alone. As he enters the carriage, he sees it's empty, although he still sits the furthest seat away from the door. He rests his head in his hands, baffled at how he is losing time whenever his mind is distracted.

"I can't be that distracted that I lose all sense of reality," he tells himself. "Maybe I should have stayed home."

The train makes a stop. A young couple enters the carriage and sit a few seats down, much to Michael's annoyance. Michael doesn't pay them any attention and turns to face away from them. He begins to think about his will and if it needs to be updated, but his train of thought is interrupted when he hears an argument.

"NO! I told you you're not going without me!"

Michael tries to ignore the bickering couple, but the young lady looks over at Michael as if to silently plead for help. However, Michael does not look in her direction. Instead, he closes his eyes and tries to return to his own thoughts, but the fight became louder until he hears a slap. Michael opens his eyes and rises to his feet in anger. The culprit is looking up at him in a disdainful manner.

"What, old man?" the youth yells at Michael.

Michael looks over at the young lady who is holding the left side of her face and painstakingly avoiding eye contact.

Michael takes a step towards the young man, who stands up and pulls out a knife. "What you gonna do, old man?" he shouts, waving the knife in the air to keep Michael at bay.

Michael says nothing as he takes another step towards the guy.

"Why don't you leave this woman alone?" he murmurs, his anger building.

"Why don't you mind your own business, old man?" is the youths retort.

"Why don't you make me?" Michael is pissed.

The kid tries to swipe at Michael with the knife., but he dodges the blade with ease and is unafraid of the weapon.

"This generation, I swear," Michael muses, shaking his head in dismay. He flicks the knife nonchalantly. "Always resorting to weapons because you're too afraid of getting your arse whipped."

Annoyed, the young man lunges forward with his arm outstretched and tries to stab Michael, but he uses an inside crescent kick to disable his assailant and knocks the knife out of his hands. Shocked by what Michael has just done, the young man throws up his hands and takes a few steps backwards.

"I'm sorry! Please don't hurt me!"

"Don't apologise to me; apologise to her," Michael says, pointing towards the young lady.

"I'm sorry, babe. It won't happen again."

As the train begins to slow down for the next stop, Michael retrieves the knife so it's in safe hands. The young man is quick to exit the carriage and gives Michael the middle finger in triumph before he runs away alone. Michael shakes his head, approaches the carriage door and drops the knife down the gap that separates the train door from the platform. He sighs, then as the train starts to move again towards its final destination, he glances over at the young lady. She is still holding her reddened left cheek and her hair covers the other half of her face so he can't see her features. Michael picks up his work bag and approaches the train door, waiting to exit at the next stop. As the train comes to a halt and the door opens, he hears a soft, shaky female voice say, "Thank you."

Michael slightly turns his head towards the lady.

"You're welcome," he replies, then he leaves the train and joins the crowd in the subway making their way to work.

Like marching ants, the hundreds of people surrounding Michael regimentally march towards work. Some are wearing headphones and listening to music to distract them from their daily lives. Others are talking on their mobile phones, trying to stay in touch with family, friends or work, totally oblivious to their surroundings. Michael sees an elderly lady trying to make her way through the crowd to her platform, but no one slows down to let her pass. Michael does and being bigger and taller than most he unintentionally creates a domino effect as everyone else also stops.

"Thank you," the old lady says gratefully as she smiles at him.

As the crowd nears the end of the subway, they all step onto the escalators to take them up to the city centre. A homeless man is at the top of the escalators begging the pedestrians for some small change. Michael does his best to manoeuvre around the foot traffic so he can avoid the homeless man. When he reaches the top of the escalators the homeless man is nowhere in sight. Michael makes his way out of the train station and breaks away from the crowd, then as he readjusts the position of his bag his left arm is grabbed.

He turns around to find the homeless man clinging to him.

"Has anyone told you that you have a strong aura?" he asks Michael as he lets go of his arm.

"No."

"It is very fascinating to see," the man continues while taking a closer look at Michael. "God must favour you."

"I dunno about that!" Michael retorts, annoyed.

"I don't mean to offend; it's just that auras like yours are rare. They say a person with a strong aura has a strong soul," the homeless man says, pointing towards Michael's chest.

Michael is sceptical, but he asks the man, "And what do you believe?"

"I believe an aura strong as yours is singing."

Michael is amused by this and offers a small laugh. "Singing? Why and to who?"

The man leans in towards Michael with a smile and replies, "The soul sings to the angels asking for help."

Michael is shocked by this. "Who are you?" he asks as he takes a step closer to the man. "And don't you want change or something instead of giving me a free spiritual reading?"

"Oh," the man lights up. "Yes please, if you have some change," and he holds out open palms.

Michael shakes his head then he reaches into his bag, pulls out his wallet and debates whether to proffer a twenty or fifty dollar note. He removes the fifty but as he turns back around the homeless man has disappeared.

Puzzled, Michael places the money back in his wallet and puts it back into his bag. *This is turning out to be such a weird day*, he thinks to himself as he makes his way to work.

Arriving at one of the taller buildings, he walks into the foyer and enters an elevator. Whilst in the elevator he takes in a deep breath as if to prepare himself to be someone else, a happier person with no personal issues. The elevator doors open, he takes one step out and exhales.

Michael is greeted by his peers. Like a royal he smiles, nods and waves at everyone he passes. He finds his seat and unloads his work bag, connects his laptop to the desk station and waits for his monitor to load up. While doing this he recalls the exact words from the doctor: *"There's no easy way to say this Michael, but I'm afraid it is Stage 2 prostate cancer."*

His computer beeps at him as it requests a password to open his desktop. He leans in, types the password and hits 'Enter'. As he does this the computer screen goes blank and starts to malfunction. The screen flickers from black to white then white to black. Michael gives his monitor a tap on the side. As he does this the following words begin to form on the screen.

Don't give in, fight!

Michael sits upright in his chair, then looks around to see if anyone else is experiencing this. The writing then changes and the message shocks Michael to his core.

God…has…work…for…you!

Michael jumps to his feet and falls backwards over his chair. The screen then flickers back and forth and reboots to his desktop. Shaken, Michael gets back to his feet and looks at his computer, but the writing has disappeared. Still taken back by what he has seen, he gathers his belongings and repacks his computer into his bag. He then storms out looking for the elevators, keeping his head down and trying to remain unnoticed. Unfortunately, a few co-workers try to greet him as he passes by. Michael doesn't stop; instead, he ignores them. When he reaches the elevators he presses the button repeatedly, hoping for an immediate arrival. He can hear conversation from his peers around the corner coming closer and closer. He hits the down button even faster.

"Come on, come on! Hurry up!" he mutters while continuing to press the button and looking at what level the elevator is currently on.

Level 14. Almost here. Level 15.

"Finally!" he says as the doors open to reveal an empty lift. He enters as fast as he can and presses the 'door close' button as he wants the elevator to himself. As the doors shut, he breathes a sigh of relief.

"What is going on with me?" he wonders, rubbing his temples. He arrives in the lobby and makes his way back through the crowded subway. As he brushes past anyone who he should find in his path people mutter swear words and others ask him to slow down. Now at his station he waits patiently for his train, then he looks over at the next platform and sees another person intently watching him. Michael realises it's the homeless man he saw earlier.

"You!" he mumbles to himself.

Michael hears his train coming through the tunnel. He urgently looks around to see if there is another path to the other platform.

"Whatever is happening with me, you are at the centre of it all!" he shouts out loud across the tracks. As he tries to make his way to some nearby stairs, he looks over and notices the man is no longer on the platform.

"What?" he exclaims as he stops, then as he starts to go back down the stairs he comments, "I must be losing my mind."

He returns to the platform just as his train arrives. He waits for everyone inside the train to exit, then he slowly makes his way inside the carriage. He sits down and exhales exhaustedly with his eyes closed.

"Doors are now closing," the speakers in the train announce.

As Michael reopens his eyes, he looks through the window and sees the homeless man waving back at him from the platform Michael was just on.

"What?" Michael cries as he rises to his feet. "No, stop!"

He tries to open the doors, but the train is beginning to move.

"No, wait!" He tries harder to open the doors, but with no success.

As the train gains momentum, Michael runs towards the next train carriage to keep the stranger in his sight.

"PLEASE, WHO ARE YOU?"

The stranger only smiles and keeps waving at Michael until he is met solidly with the end of the train carriage wall.

Michael picks himself up off the floor and looks through the carriage window, but the homeless man has again disappeared.

All the passengers on the train are staring at him like he's crazy and keeping their distance from him. Michael sits down on the nearest seat, his whole body slumped in defeat. He then removes his work bag from his shoulder, places it beside him and leans forward with his head in his hands.

What is going on?

First, there was the young lady on the train, then his encounter with the homeless man and his computer talking to him through a message on his screen.

Did that actually happen, or did I imagine that? he wonders as he sits upright and looks out the window of the train. *What does it all mean?*

While he is trying to piece it all together, he again loses track of time.

"Next stop Guildford!" the train speaker announces.

Flustered, he retrieves his bag and stands at the door waiting for the train to stop. When it arrives at his destination, he exits the carriage and hastily makes his way to his car. Sitting in his vehicle, he closes his eyes and in his mind, he sees the stranger on the train platform smiling and waving at him.

Who is he? And why can't I stop thinking of him? It has to mean something.

He shakes his head to rid himself of the memory, then he starts his car and drives off.

Chapter 3

The Red Horse

The sky begins to darken, and an ominous rumbling can be heard from the heavens, as if a stern warning to the Earthlings below. Michael checks his phone for the time as well as any unchecked messages. Instead, he sees two missed calls from work.

He rolls his eyes before placing his phone down and continuing to drive. He parks at the oval next to the church he once visited and contemplates going inside again. Instead, he sits back and again goes over today's events in his mind. Exhausted, he quickly falls asleep, so deep in his own thoughts.

In his subconscious darkness is all around him. He notices smoke beginning to rise from the ground before him, while in the background are the silhouettes of demolished buildings.

"What is this?" he wonders as the smoke begins to take shape and colour. "It looks like a red horse."

The smoky red horse now begins to move slowly, almost fluidly. As it turns its gaze towards Michael, it grunts and blows thick white smoke from its nostrils. Michael takes a backward step as the dark red horse begins to bleed all over.

"What is going on?"

The horse begins to stomp its front hooves at Michael, trying to intimidate him. Michael doesn't retreat. Instead, he tries to observe the horse, but the animal is agitated by his curiosity and charges at Michael.

"Aargh!" he cries as he begins to run, then he is disturbed from his sleep by a stranger outside his car.

"Sorry, I didn't mean to startle you!."

Michael looks around, disorientated, and notices that the stranger is a priest.

"You're in your car. Well, I hope this is your car," the priest jokes, but Michael doesn't laugh. "I'm sorry," the priest apologises. "Are you lost, or can I help you with something?"

"No, I was just passing through," Michael responds, shrugging off the priest's help.

Recognising his voice, the priest asks, "Hey, were you at the confessional last night?"

Michael panics and starts his car.

"Wait!" the priest cries, but Michael hastily reverses his car and drives off. He glances in his rear-view mirror and sees the priest watching him in dismay. He soon arrives back home, and notices Kelly's car is already in the garage and the boys school bags are hanging on the hooks close by.

"Must be Friday," Michael says out loud, trying to regain some sanity by establishing what day of the week it is. He joins Kelly in the kitchen and as he helps her pack away the groceries he asks, "So, how was your day, gorgeous?"

"Good, but I was worried about you. I really don't think you should've gone to work today."

"I was fine, hun," Michael lies, then he turns to Kelly and places a hand over hers. "You don't need to worry about me, okay?"

"Okay," Kelly replies with a nod.

Michael kisses his wife on the forehead and starts to walk to their bedroom to get out of his work clothes, but something catches his eye on the television in the lounge, so he walks over to the screen.

"Babe! You, okay?" Kelly calls.

When Michael doesn't reply, she walks over to him and asks, "Babe, what's going on?"

She moves Michael aside to take a look at what is troubling her husband. She can see that he is overcome with fear, so she tries to change the channel for him, but every channel she flicks to seems to be televising the same event.

"Babe?" Kelly calls, trying to get her husband's attention. "BABE!"

"Yes?" Michael replies as he looks at her.

"What is going on in here?" she asks as she gently rubs the side of his head.

"I have seen this before," he whispers as he turns his attention back to the TV and turns the volume up.

Both Kelly and Michael watch the news. The screen shows a mushroom like red cloud in the shape of a horse over Vatican City.

"The St Peter's Basilica was just attacked," the reporter announces. *"It has been completely destroyed and all that remains is this strange cloud that is hovering over the ruins."*

"What do you mean you've seen this before?" Kelly asks Michael, trying to stay calm.

"I...I dreamt this," Michael manages to reply.

"You dreamt that Saint Peter's Basilica was going to be attacked?"

"No! I dreamt that!" Michael says, pointing at the horse-like cloud on the screen. "It's as if someone is trying to tell me something."

"Who's trying to tell you something?" Kelly responds, her voice a little shaky.

"I don't know...but that cloud is bad news!" Michael says confidently.

"I feel like there's more that you're not telling me," Kelly turns to her husband, but

Michael walks away from the TV and makes his way towards their bedroom.

"Where are you going?" Kelly asks as she follows him.

"I'm getting changed, I might go out for a quick jog. I just need to clear my head."

"It is about to rain, Michael. Can't you hear that rumbling?" she asks, pointing skywards.

"I won't be too long. I just need to think," he replies while he begins to undress and put on his favourite hooded jumper.

"You better take your phone," she insists, then she storms off without waiting for her husband's response.

Unclear as to why his wife is agitated, he sits down and sighs deeply before he slowly puts on his joggers and heads for the front door. Stepping outside he sees why his wife is angry. The sky is dark, thunder is rumbling all around and lightning flashes are everywhere.

"Just a quick jog," he tells himself as he starts to walk down his street towards the oval.

Chapter 4

Judgement

Michael is in deep thought, contemplating the news report and his dream. *What does that cloud mean?*

At the end of the street, he crosses the road to the oval. Drops of rain fall on the top of his head so he throws his hood on and sees people on the oval packing away the night market.

He watches for a moment before he begins to jog around the oval, keeping to himself and avoiding making eye contact with the busy stall holders. A bored little girl catches his attention as he jogs along the footpath towards the people sheltering under a pergola from the rain. She waves at him, and he politely waves back before he begins a second lap. Suddenly the sky stops rumbling and everything goes dark as the streetlights switch off, leaving an eerie silence. Michael stops jogging and looks around, but he can barely see in front of him.

"What the…?" he says out loud, then there is a deafening crack of thunder which makes everyone seek cover. The sky lights up turning night into day as the lightning storm begins. As Michael runs for shelter, lightning strikes near him left and right, as if he's magnetic. He does his best to dodge it, then a lightning strike in front of him stops him in his tracks. Losing his balance, he stumbles over and crashes to the ground. When he looks up he notices hundreds of lightning bolts striking the earth. Mesmerised by this sight he forgets the danger he is in until he hears a cry for help. He looks for the location of the screams and sees the young girl that waved to him earlier trying to help an elderly man who is trapped under some stall debris.

Michael runs over to her without a second thought. The lightning seems to be following him, striking beside him and behind him but not in front, as if directing him. When he reaches the elderly man lying helpless on the ground he tells Michael, "Take her!"

"No, Dad!" the young girl yells, but Michael picks her up and says, "Let's go."

"No, we can't leave him!" she cries as she flails about in Michael's arms.

"I'll come back for him, I promise."

The girl calms down after Michael's promise and rests her head on his shoulder.

She begins to sob and feels her rescuer's racing heart as her hands are placed over his chest. *He is just as scared as I am,* she realises.

Michael clutches her tighter and runs faster as the lightning eases up. He manages to get to the crowd under the shelter, and a woman reaches her arms out towards the girl.

"Autumn!"

"Mum!" she cries as she falls into her arms.

Michael was about to return for the elderly man when the skies went dark again, and all the lightning stopped. Everyone cautiously came out from the shelter and looked up at the sky in amazement.

"It's stopped," one of the bystanders exclaim.

"Hmm," Michael thinks to himself as he gazes up at the now calm sky. He walks over to the elderly man and lifts up the debris and a wooden beam which had trapped his leg. The man gingerly stands up and hobbles over to his family.

"Dad!" Autumn yells out as she hugs her father.

"Ooh, not so tight," he gasps, clearly feeling pain.

Something catches Michael's attention in the dark sky. A dull glow is beginning to emit from the thick clouds above. The sky begins to light up again, only this time the lightning surges towards the glowing clouds.

Michael looks on baffled while everyone else scurries back to the shelter yelling, "It's starting again!"

The once dull glow is now a blinding light in the sky and a sombre buzz can be heard from within it, like millions of angry bees waiting to attack.

Michael is spooked as this noise gets louder. He takes a few steps back, ready to run at a moment's notice, then the loudest crack of thunder explodes through the night sky followed by a swift bolt of lightning. It strikes Michael in the head and his limbs stiffen out from the electrocution. The lightning pulses down from the sky and passes repeatedly through his entire body while everyone watches on in horror. Some scream while others turn their heads away, unable to watch.

"STOP IT!" Autumn yells out hysterically, unable to bear watching her rescuer suffer.

As she yells the lighting stops and Michael slumps lifeless to the ground.

"Is it over?" several people whisper, looking anxiously up at the silent sky.

"Mister!" Autumn yells as she races towards Michael's body which is emitting smoke.

"Autumn, no!" her mother cries. "Don't touch him!"

They all surround Michael and gaze upon him sadly, some crying while others try to comprehend what just took place.

"MICHAEL! MICHAEL!"

They all look in the direction of this faint call and see a lady frantically looking for someone. "MICHAEL!"

Autumn's father tries to get the lady's attention by waving his arms at her. "Hello? Can we help you?"

"I'm looking for my husband," Kelly replies as she approaches the crowd. "He was wearing a black hoodie and long black pants."

The crowd looks down at the dishevelled, burnt black hoodie the lightning victim is wearing and exchange worried looks.

Autumn's mother walks over to Kelly and reaches for her hand, then she solemnly leads her to the man lying motionless on the ground.

"NO!" Kelly cries, her heart sinking as she kneels beside her husband. Bursting into tears she places her hands on Michael's chest and croaks, "What happened?"

"One of the lightning bolts got him," one of the bystanders answers.

Kelly sobs more as she studies her husband's burnt body. Overcome with pain, she places her hands over his face.

"He saved me from the lightning," Autumn told Kelly, trying to comfort her with Michael's courage.

Kelly feels the artery in Michael's neck. "I can't find a pulse. Has anyone called an ambulance?"

"It happened so— "

"Please someone call an ambulance," Kelly pleads as she starts to cry over Michael's body and whispers to him, "I told you not to go. Why didn't you listen?"

"The ambulance is on their way," one member of the crowd announces, then the silence is broken by hundreds of emergency sirens echoing throughout their small suburb. Ambulances, fire trucks and police cars were out in force. Captivated by the display of red and blue flashing lights and wailing sirens, the crowd watches on.

Kelly stands as one ambulance detours from the road and heads onto the oval.

"Over here!" the crowd yells as they wave down the ambulance.

Kelly kneels back down and whispers to Michael, "Hold on, babe,"

Everyone makes way for the ambulance in a mad scramble. The officers inside the vehicle look at each other in disbelief when they see a lifeless body on the ground with smoke still issuing from it. One of the officers jumps out of the ambulance and begins CPR on Michael while the other gathers the defibrillator.

"One…two…three…four," the medic counts as he begins his CPR compressions on the victim's chest.

Crying uncontrollably, Kelly watches on, helpless and hoping for any sign of life from her husband.

"I'm getting nothing here. Are you ready with the defib?"

"Almost done!" his partner responds, then he places a pad over Michael's chest and the other under his rib region.

"Okay, everyone get back, make some space," the medic shouts, then once they are clear he presses the 'Shock' button when instructed by the electronic device. Michael's body jumps and jolts, then when the shock stops his body lies still again.

The ambulance officers repeat the process again, but they are still unable to revive him.

"One more time and that's it," one of the ambulance officers says quietly to the other, but Kelly overhears them.

"What?" she says numbly.

The two medics nod at each other, approving the next shock for Michael.

"Stand clear," the defibrillator announces. The officer pauses for a moment as if saying a prayer to himself first, then he pushes the 'Shock' button and Michael's body jolts for the final time.

"Please, babe, come back to me!" Kelly yells at Michael.

The defibrillator overloads and as sparks fly from it everyone ducks for cover. The ambulance also surges with power. Its lights and siren turn on, startling everyone around Michael's body, which is still jolting.

"That's too long, turn it off!" one medic yells at the other in panic.

When they try to unplug Michael, they are shocked themselves. One officer is flung through the air, colliding with the back of the ambulance, while the other is sent flying towards the screaming bystanders. The overloaded defibrillator explodes, and everyone shields themselves from the errant sparks before this small light show comes to an end.

Michael's body is once again lying motionless on the ground.

"MICHAEL!" Kelly cries as she rushes back to her husband and hovers over his body. She gently touches him, checking if it's safe or if any electrical current remains within his body.

"Michael!" Kelly shouts, shaking him for a response. "Michael!"

Everyone bows their heads, sad that Michael is no longer with them, then they check on each other. They help the shaken ambulance officers back to their feet, while Kelly cries over her husband's body.

A Christmas jingle comes on the radio while everyone looks on dumbfoundedly, then there is a faint noise from the defibrillator which seems louder than the radio music.

"Beep!"

A heartbeat.

"Beep!"

"Help him!" Kelly yells to the ambulance officers. One applies an oxygen mask over Michael's mouth while the other retrieves the gurney from the ambulance.

Kelly is overwhelmed with joy; her beaming smile is felt by everyone around her.

The bystanders give her a comforting hug and then she feels a smaller, gentler hug. She looks down and sees Autumn smiling up at her. Kelly smiles back.

Michael is still unconscious as he is placed into the ambulance. An officer tells Kelly, "We'll take him to the hospital, and you can meet him there."

Kelly agrees and jogs towards her car, anxious to be at the hospital as soon as Michael arrives.

Back on the oval, the crowd is dispersing. As they begin to leave, Autumn notices the burnt grass where Michael's body once lay. She walks around the markings like a game, trying not to fall off the outline.

"Autumn, let's go!" Her mother calls from a distance.

"Mum! Mum! There're big wings on the ground!"

"Let's go, Autumn," Her other repeats in a sterner voice.

Autumn runs towards her mother.

The outline of Michael's body is burnt into the grass like the outline of a homicide victim. However, around his silhouette was a pair of fully outstretched wings, like those of an angel.

Chapter 5

Spiritual Healing

The ambulance slowly approaches the emergency entrance of the chaotic hospital where the nurses are busy triaging all the casualties of the night's storm event. They quickly open up the back of the ambulance and roll him out of the vehicle and into the hospital.

"He was struck by lightning and had no pulse," the ambulance officer explains. "We administered CPR and defibrillation. On the final attempt, the AED exploded…"

"What?" the head nurse, Natalie, exclaims, surprised. "Then what happened?"

The two ambulance officers exchange a look.

"Then the patient produced a pulse," the medic concludes.

"Wait, he produced a pulse straight after the explosion?"

"Yes!" they reply in unison.

Natalie is taken back by the story, but she makes her notes and places it in Michael's patient folder on the edge of his stretcher, "He is not the only lightning victim tonight. Welcome to our slice of hell," she exclaims, gesturing towards the busy nurses attending to the other victims. "We have another one!" Natalie shouts into the masses, pushing Michael towards the emergency ward.

Two other nurses scramble to assist her.

"Whoa! This one is far worse than the others," one nurse observes, seeing Michael's charred body.

"Yes, we need to be careful with him," Natalie says. "It's unclear what type of damage his body has gone through. As he's stable, we need to rinse and clean him down first to understand what we're working with. When we clean him ensure that it is with a damp sterile cloth and you must dab, not wipe the wounds. Is that clear?"

"Yes, Natalie."

The nurses rinse his body down and gently wipe his wounds clean using the dab method, then one exclaimed, "Huh?"

"What is it?" the head nurse asks.

"I could have sworn this cut was deeper," she says, pointing towards a small cut on Michael's rib cage.

The other nurses stare at her as if she's crazy, so she shrugs it off and continues to carefully wipe the patient down.

Once Michael is fully clean, the nurses assess him, noting every cut and bruise on his body for his patient record. He is then covered almost from head to toe with polyvinyl chloride film to treat his charred body and then transferred to the burns ward.

"Patient is stable with minor cuts," Natalie announces, "however, he is still comatose. Attempting the trapezius pinch." When she pinches Michael's trapezius muscle she gets a reaction almost instantly. "Normal flexion," she writes into his patient file. "Four on the Glasgow Coma Scale."

Kelly and the kids are directed to the front desk of the burns ward as the nurses finish off Michael's paperwork.

"Excuse me, my name is Kelly Valor. My husband Michael was struck by lightning and brought here. Is he okay?" she asks anxiously.

"Mrs Valor, he's in a coma, but he is stable and has been taken to his room, you may see him as you are family but then we must let him rest."

"I understand. Which room is he in?"

"Go down to the Burns ward and you will find him in room 11" the nurse directs

When they arrive, they find Natalie making her final checks and observations. "Are you his family?"

"Yes. How is he?"

Dropping her voice, Natalie murmurs to Kelly, "He was unresponsive verbally, so we tested him further physically and he responded." Seeing a sign of relief on Kelly's face, Natalie gently holds her forearm and warns her, "He's not out of the woods just yet, so we still need to give him some rest. I will leave you alone, but I will return once visiting time is over."

After the head nurse leaves, Hudson and Isaiah try to wake their father.

"Dad! Dad! Daaaaad!"

"He needs to rest, boys" Kelly says gently, trying hard not to seem too worried in front of the kids.

"What happened to Dad?" Hudson asks.

"Yeah, what happened?" Isaiah asks inquisitively.

Kelly kneels to their eye level and says, "You remember all of the lightning you saw earlier?"

"Yes," Isaiah says with wide eyes. "I hated that!"

"Well, your dad was…" Kelly begins to explain but the words are proving difficult to get out.

"Was what?" Hudson demands.

"He was struck by one of those lightning bolts, love," she replies as a single tear runs down her cheek.

All three kids gasped in shock and fall silent as they try to process what this could mean for their father.

"Will he be okay, Mum?" Isaiah asks in a soft voice.

"Yes, baby, he will. He just needs some rest to get his strength back."

While her brothers are holding their father's hand, Emma quietly asks her mother, "Are you just saying that or will he be okay?"

"The nurses say he is in a coma, but he's responsive which is a good sign."

"Maybe we should give him time to recoup then, like the nurse says?" Emma suggests, then hugging her mum tightly she whispers, "Dad is strong, he will wake from this."

Kelly nods, then as Emma releases her she said to her sons, "Well come on, you two. We better let him rest now."

Both boys hopped off their father's bedside, then Isaiah kissed his father's hands. Seeing this act of affection from his brother Hudson rushes back and does the same thing.

"Get better soon, Dad!" he tells him, then he rushes to his mother who is standing by the door with the others.

Kelly senses something; a feeling as though someone is watching them. She turns around and looks back at her husband, hoping it's him but unfortunately, he is still unconscious. She then looks towards the windows and sees nothing except the dark night outside.

"What's wrong, Mum?" Hudson asks.

"It's nothing, hun," Kelly says as they leave Michael's room.

Once they had gone, the homeless man Michael encountered at the train station emerges from behind the curtains and walks over to Michael's bedside, his face stricken with grief and remorse.

"What have I done?" he mutters to himself.

Chapter 6

What dwells beneath

"Another murder scene in our northern suburbs tonight," a television in the nurse's station outside Michael's room blares, capturing everyone's attention. *"The mother and father leave behind two young children: a six-year-old boy and an eleven-year-old girl."*

"Wat is the world coming to?!" a young nurse says with a sad shake of the head.

"The two police constables called to the crime scene are also missing in action," the news reporter continued. *"The constables called the ambulance but were not at the scene when the medics arrived. We now cross live to Police Sergeant Andrew Mourning who is making an announcement."*

Consulting his notes, the sergeant said, *"It is now apparent that the crime scene officers attended this evening is being treated as a homicide. I can also confirm that we have two officers missing from the scene who we believe were first to respond: Constable Peter Dolan and Constable Megan Sacks. A search is underway for both officers."*

"Did they have something to do with the murders?" a news reporter yells out.

"They are members of our Police family and at this stage are being treated as witnesses to this heinous crime. We need information and clarity around the events of this evening, and they may have answers for the victims' family." The sergeant looks up into the cameras, his face stoic, his shoulders squared perfectly in the frame: this is not his first rodeo. "The victims and the families of everyone involved are in our thoughts and prayers tonight. Thank you.",

"Sir! Sir!" all the reporters yell as they try their hardest to get in another question, but Sergeant Mourning abruptly packs up his paperwork and leaves the podium. His image on the screen is replaced by beaming photographs of Constables Sacks and Dolan, immaculate uniforms and bright eyes. Along the bottom the screen the Crimestoppers phone number and website scroll in a loop.

The head nurse turns the television off and commands, "Alright everyone, back to work." Outside the hospital Kelly and the kids bicker with each other.

"Mum, I wanted chips!" Isaiah cries as they exit the hospital.

"You can't have chips from that stupid machine, they'll rot your teeth away," she yells back at Isaiah.

When he cries, Kelly feels guilty, so she kneels and gives him a cuddle. "I'll tell you what, if you're good on the drive home, we'll get something to eat along the way."

Isaiah's face lights up. "Okay."

"Emma, can you take them to the car?" Kelly asks she stands in front of the parking meter.

Emma nods and cradles both her brothers saying, "Come on, boys."

Kelly pays for her parking ticket and sees the kids waiting in the car for her. She begins to walk along the footpath but is suddenly inexplicably spooked by the person she sees walking towards her. The man is almost dragging himself along, as if he's in a trance, his long face slack and expressionless. He isn't moving aside for Kelly on the footpath, so she makes way for him as he slowly passes her. Kelly almost gags at his stench; it's like rotting flesh and week-old rubbish which has been left to sit in the sun. His clothes, she noticed, are filthy and tattered with holes everywhere. Kelly swiftly rushes to the safety of her car and starts the engine.

"What's wrong, Mum?" Hudson asks.

"Nothing, all good," she reassures Hudson while keeping a watchful eye on the strange man as she drives off. When they arrive at the boom gate, Kelly is quick to place the ticket into the machine. She can see the dishevelled man is getting closer to the end of the footpath, just at the same time as the machine rejects the ticket.

"Come on, come on!" Kelly whispers to herself, trying to keep a level head. She pushes the ticket back into the machine and it thinks about it for a bit. Finally, the boom gate acknowledges the ticket and lifts. Unfortunately, the scary man walks across the road directly in their path, preventing Kelly from driving off.

"Whoa! Is he a real zombie?" Hudson yells as the family watches the stranger through the windscreen. The man seems to be awake, but his body reacts in a frightening manner, twitching as he walks. Slowly he paces across the road, not registering his surroundings at all. His face has a blank look as if someone else is driving his body.

Now able to drive away, Kelly does so with haste while the man continues his journey. He hobbles for some time down the dark footpath leading to an underpass bridge dubbed 'Homeless Cove' by the locals.

A disturbing grumbling sound emits from the Cove, get louder as the man enters the underpass. He bumps into other figures like himself who moan and groan monstrously. Their eyes glow ominously red through the night and a huge, dark figure is seen sitting in front of a fire.

"Aah, another child has joined the ranks," –a grotesque creature says in a sickly voice as the fire changes to blue flames and disintegrates into powder. The creature places powder into a pouch, and hands it over to two people "Another batch to hand out. This time target busier crowds. Like the night scene."

"As you wish, Master," they both reply, then they kneel and bow to the dark figure in a worshiping manner.

"Go!" he commands, shooing them both away.

Police Constables Peter Dolan and Megan Sacks rise to do the dark figure's bidding, still dressed in their uniforms. They march away silently, obeying the commands of the unknown creature and not questioning the significance of the mysterious powder they now hold.

Chapter 7

Godsend

A nurse holds up the patient file at the foot of the bed. "One, two weeks," she marks off before placing the file back in the holder, then she opens the curtains, letting in the morning sunlight. "That's better," she says to herself, and leaves the room.

The toilet door opens, and a man appears and checks if it's all clear. He walks out and closes Michael's door slightly, then he sits by his bedside.

"Yes, I'm still here. You can't get rid of me that easily," he tells the unconscious figure. "It's been a fortnight, why aren't you awake? The others have already woken up, why haven't you? Maybe..." he whispers as if unsure of himself, "No, no, I can't think like that. I am certain of you."

A slight twitch from Michael's hand interrupts the man's train of thought.

"Huh?" he gasps. He waits for any further sign of movement; his anticipation builds, but in vain: nothing more happens. Instead, he hears Kelly saying good morning to the nurses and the sound of the boys chattering boisterously down the hall, on their way to visit their dad.

"Great!" he grumbles out loud. "This isn't over!" he tells Michael before concealing himself again.

"Hello?" Kelly says as she enters Michael's room, for she was sure she heard a voice.

The boys race in rambunctiously and immediately jump to their dad's bedside.

"Ssh!" Kelly scolds them. "Boys, there are other patients in this hospital."

Emma sighs and rolls her eyes as she sits down. Both boys are apologetic and sit down next to their sister.

"Mum, how long now until Dad wakes up?" Isaiah moans.

"I don't know, hun. I'll speak with the doctor today and ask."

"It's nearly Christmas and Dad promised he'd put up the Christmas lights."

Isaiah's words echo deep within Michael's subconscious, particularly the word 'promised'. It echoes over and over within Michael, as if it is a duty that holds him to account. It burrows so deep that it disrupts his subconscious.

"I PROMISE!" Michael screams as he finally awakes.

"Dad!" both boys yell as they rush to him and jump on his bed for a big dad hug.

"What? Where am I?" Michael asks, disorientated as he gives his boys hugs.

Kelly rushes to the door and screams at the nearest nurse. "HE'S AWAKE!" then rushes back for her own hug from Michael. Soon the whole family is hugging and squeezing one another..

"Okay, okay," Michael begins. "I need to know what's happening."

The doctor enters the room to find the entire family are smiling while Michael is still trying to collect himself.

"Right!" the doctor begins. "Welcome back, Michael. Now, we've have taken some scans of your entire body, as we needed to see the extent of the damage. I'm glad to say that, quite miraculously, you're in good health."

"Uh, Doctor, what about my cancer?" Michael murmurs, but Emma hears him.

The doctor flicks through Michael's file, then he says quietly, "I see you were diagnosed with prostate cancer a few weeks back."

"*A few weeks!*" Michael breathes, stunned and up till now totally unaware of how long he was out for.

"Yes, it's been two weeks since your accident. Sorry, I should have started with that," he laughs awkwardly. "Look - the scans we conducted should have picked up your cancer. Fortunately, I am not seeing the cancer in these scans."

"That's great news!" Kelly smiles and hugs Michael who seems to be having some trouble grasping his new lease on life.

"Um, should I get a re-scan, Doctor?" Michael asks. "Just to be sure."

"You're welcome to get a re-scan, but we have done numerous scans and tests while you were under. We've been taking and testing bloods and have charted every move you've made. You name it, we've tested it," the Doctor concludes with a slightly nervous smile.

"How could this be?" Michael asks, puzzled.

"We actually don't know how this is possible," the doctor conceded. "We're all just as baffled as you are. Maybe the lightning cured you," he jokes, but Michael takes it seriously.

"Do you think that's possible?"

"Absolutely not. Up until now, I thought getting hit by a lightning bolt would kill you, so you're a walking miracle in more ways than one, my friend."

"So, when am I cleared to go home, Doctor?"

"Yes, when can Dad come home?" both boys ask.

"Well, I've just conducted my final tests, so I am happy to discharge you today if you like—"

"Yes," Michael interrupts the doctor. "Yes, I'd like that very much!"

Michael and Kelly smile at each other. He invites Kelly to come closer and reaches out for her hands. She clenches his hands tightly, relieved their darkest days are now behind them.

"Right, well, I better be off," the doctor announces to the family. "Happy to know you're feeling better. If you have any mishaps or if you feel disoriented or unwell in any way, please contact the hospital and not your local GP."

"Yes, yes will do, Doc," Michael replied. "Thank you."

"Yay! Dad is coming home!" Hudson and Isaiah cried in delight.

"I don't suppose anyone has some clothes for me?" Michael asks.

Kelly laughs and looks at Emma who rolls her eyes.

"What? What's going on?" Michael asks.

"Mum always brings a bag of your belongings when we come to visit you," Emma mocks her mum.

"Whose crazy now?" Kelly replied. "I always knew you were going to wake up, Michael, I just didn't know when, so every day I brought your bag."

"Wow! Thanks gorgeous! I guess I'll go and get changed then," Michael says as he slowly gets out of bed.

"Be careful," Kelly warns, trying to help him. As the blood rushes back down throughout his entire body, Michael is sluggish and a little disorientated.

"I'm okay, I'm okay," he reassures Kelly. "Let me sit here for a bit." Michael sits on the edge of the bed and asks, "Can I have some water?"

"Yes, of course," Kelly says as she reaches for the jug of water on the bedside table and pours him a glass.

At first he sips it gingerly, but then he gulps it all down, his thirst feeling almost insatiable.

"Ahh!" he exclaims as he finishes his drink and hands the glass back to his wife.

"You sure you're okay?" Kelly asks with concern.

"Yeah, I'm okay," Michael reassures her as he stands steadily on his own, then he slowly makes his way towards the toilet. As he enters the room, he glances at himself in the mirror and sees another man behind the toilet door with a grin on his face.

Spooked, he looks behind the door, but no one is there. He looks back at the mirror and only sees himself.

"What was that about?" he wonders to himself as he closes the door behind him. He begins to get undressed, but his gown proves difficult to get off, tied as it is behind his back in a nurses knot. He reaches behind him, trying to untie it, but feels something abnormal on his skin.

"What the…?" he begins, then he turns his back towards the mirror and pulls on the string to untie his robe, revealing two long slits on his back. Each slit starts from the shoulder blade and goes all the way down to his lower back lumbar region. He presses his fingertips against the slits to see if there is any pain, but there is none to speak of so he continues to feel around the slits, which look like incisions. He pokes and prods and slides a finger into the incision, but again there is no pain, so he explores deeper and is shocked at how deep his finger goes.

"What is this?" he exclaims, then Kelly knocks on the door to check on him.

Startled he takes his finger out of the slit and looks in the mirror.

"I'm okay," he reassures her as he quickly gets dressed. "I'm coming out now."

"Okay," Kelly responds, then she tells the kids, "Your father's coming out soon, then we can all go home."

"What is this whole cancer thing the doctor mentioned?" Emma asks her mother.

"Um, that's something we can discuss later, okay, Hun?"

"Okay."

Kelly gives her daughter a hug, then Michael opens the door all dressed and ready to go. "Okay, whose ready to get outta here?"

"Me! Me!" the boys cry in unison.

"Okay, then let's go," he says, holding their hands.

The family leaves his room and Kelly approaches the nurse station. "We're leaving now. Is there anything you need from us before we go?"

"Nope! We have all we need, and the doctor has already signed off on everything."

"Great! Thank you," Kelly responds.

"Okay, bye," the nurse replied, waving to them as they left the hospital.

The long drive home was a quiet one. Both boys were glued to their tablets and Michael was watching the scenery passing by from the passenger seat.

"You okay, Hun?" Kelly asks.

"Yeah," he replied, still staring out the door window. "Just trying to grasp how I lost two weeks of my life after getting struck by lightning."

Kelly placed a hand on his leg. "You sure you're okay?"

Michael turns to her. "I just..." he pauses, then he whispers to Kelly hoping the kids won't hear him, "I don't know how I survived."

"Hey, just be grateful you did. I am."

Michael had forgotten that this would have also taken a toll on his family. He looks back at his kids, whom all seemed pre-occupied in their own worlds. He looks at Kelly and nods to her in agreement.

"You're right, I'm sorry." He smiles and places his hand over hers, then he continues to look out the window.

Soon they arrive at their destination and Kelly drives into the garage of their family home. "Now the house might be a little worse for wear," she warns Michael as he exits the car.

"It's fine!" Michael smiles back at his wife. "I'm just happy to be back home"

Both boys zip past him as he closes the passenger door. Emma strolls by looking at her dad accusingly before she enters their home.

"What was that about?" Michael asks Kelly as she closes the garage.

"I think she may be upset that we kept the cancer thing a secret."

"Oh!"

"Yeah, you might want to have a chat with her later."

"Maybe I'll do that now, before I relax," Michael suggests.

"Yes, the sooner the better," Kelly agrees.

Michael enters the house and makes his way to Emma's room. Her door is ajar and he can see her sitting in her chair reading a book with headphones on.

"Knock-knock!" he says as he raps on her door.

"Yes?" she says as she takes off her headphones and lays her book down.

"Mum told me that you may have heard about my cancer?" Michael said in a calm manner as he sits on the edge of her bed.

"Yes, but no one is saying anything about it," she replies with a hint of frustration.

"I know, but Mum's attitude is she doesn't like to tell someone else's story. It's my story to tell, not hers, so don't blame her."

"So can you tell me what is going on?" Emma asks.

"Yes, I can." Michael readjusts his sitting posture and tries to get comfortable. "Well, I was diagnosed with, uh, prostate cancer, last week...I mean, last month," he corrects himself as he recalls that he was in a coma for two and a half weeks. "I asked Mum not to tell you and the boys."

"Why?" Emma asks.

"Cos, I needed more time to myself to grasp what life was going to look like now that I had cancer."

"Had?" Emma was smart enough to spot the past tense.

"Good pick-up," Michael laughs. "Well, the night I wanted to figure things out was the night I went out for a jog. And..." He trails off, finding it hard to say out loud what happened next.

"You were struck by lightning." Emma prompts.

"Yes, that's right. Well, the doctor at the hospital told your Mother and I that they did a heap of scans to see the extent of the damage the lightning may have caused, but they can't find a hint of cancer. Not one bit.""

Emma's face is a mix between astounded confusion and immense relief. "Really? So it's gone?"

"Yes. I'm still trying to understand it all, but it looks like I'm in the clear."

Emma smiles at her father, then she hugs him. "That's good news. You don't have to understand anything, Dad, just take the win."

"I know, I know," Michael agrees as she releases him.

"Also I think you have some bandages on your back," Emma told him. "You may want to take them off before you go to bed."

"Okay, I will" Michael replies as he rises. "So are we good?" he asks, holding a fist out towards her, looking for a fist bump.

"We're good," she confirms with a bump and a smile.

"Good," he says, then he leaves to check on Kelly.

He finds his wife in their bedroom folding away some clean laundry whilst sitting on their bed.

"There you are!"

"Where else would I be?" Kelly jokes in response

"I've been meaning to show you something on my back," he said as he takes his shirt off.

"Whoa!" Kelly exclaims in surprise, then she rises to her feet to take a closer look. "What the hell? They're like two massive cuts," she whispers, fingering the long line from shoulder blade to waist.

"I thought I was dreaming when I first saw them," Michael tells her.

"How did you see them?" Kelly asks.

"In the mirror when I was getting dressed in the hospital."

"Huh!" Kelly says to herself, then she gently pries open a section of one of the cuts on his back and asks curiously, "Does this hurt?"

"Does what hurt? What are you doing?"

"Whoa!" Kelly gasps as she places half her hand inside the cut. "There seems to be something inside here!"

"What?" Michael yells and turns around. "You had your finger insi—" He can't finish the sentence as he begins to gag.

"Nope," Kelly replies. "I had half my hand down there."

Michael gags again only louder this time.

"Oh, please, can I have another look?" Kelly ask eagerly.

"No, stop!" Michael protests, trying to keep his back away from Kelly. "Okay, what did you feel? You know, when your hand was there?"

"When my hand was inside—" Kelly jokes.

Michael interjects sternly "Stop! Just answer. Why must you make it sound gross?"

"Okay, okay," Kelly laughs it off. "I was expecting it to be wet, being a cut but…"

"But what?"

"It felt dry, and I think I felt something soft."

"What do you mean 'soft'?" Michael asks.

"Like a feather."

"What?" Michael cries, sounding confused.

"Yeah, can I have another feel around?" Kelly asks.

"No!"

"Oh, please, please! I promise to be gentle, Michael."

"Stop making it weird," he replies, then after a moment's thought he said, "Okay, but narrate everything as it happens."

"Okay," Kelly smiles as she turns her husband around and begins to bend him over.

"Stop! You're making it weird again!" Michael protests.

"I just want you to turn around or maybe sit down on the bed while I look," Kelly says with a smile as she guides him to the bed.

"Next time just say so," Michael says as he obliges and sits on the bed with his back to his wife.

"Okay, I'm going to inspect this one. You okay with that?" Kelly says to Michael as she pokes on the left slit.

"Yes, okay."

"Half my hand is in like before and again I can feel something soft," Kelly tells him.

"Do you think it's something you can pull on?"

"I don't know if you want me to, but I can try."

"Go ahead," Michael answers.

"Okay." Kelly begins to tug on the fluffy object inside Michael. "I think I got it. Are you sure you want me to pull it out?"

"Yes, but slowly as it might hurt if you do it fast."

"Alright, I'm pulling it out now. What the…?" Kelly gasps.

"What? What is it?" Michael demands.

"See for yourself," she replies, then as she pulls the object out and extended it. Michael is stunned speechless.

"Honey, you have wings inside you!" Kelly says excitedly. "And look, they're the same colour as your hair," she jokes as she pulls the wing up to his hair. "See, grey. They match, ha-ha!"

"My hair is silver, not grey!" Michael retorts.

"I wonder how long they extend to?" Curious, Kelly pulls on the wing and stretches it as far as possible. The span is so large she has to leave the room to extend the wing out to its full extent of nearly three metres.

"Whoa!" Kelly breathes. "Does that hurt? Now the wing is fully extended?"

"That's the strangest thing!" Michael says softly. "It doesn't hurt at all. Also now that one is extended I can feel the other one in the right slit."

"Oh, we should pull them both out!" Kelly exclaims. "Here, hold on to this wing," she tells him, but the wing retracts on its own and went back into the slit. "Oops, sorry!"

"That's okay. It didn't hurt."

"Oh…my…God!" Kelly gasps.

"What?"

"Okay, don't make fun of me, but I think you have wings."

Michael snorts. "No shit!"

"No, I'm serious. Like, they're a part of you. I thought that wing was going to pull all the way out and stay out, as if it got lodged and stuck inside you somehow. But it's actually a part of you."

Kelly begins to shed a tear, much to Michael's surprise.

"What's wrong? Why are you crying?"

"What if the lightning gave you these?"

"You think that's what happened?"

Kelly nods. "Yes, and I think you were struck for a reason."

Michael doesn't know what to say to that. Instead, he quietly contemplates what this could mean.

"Don't you get it, Hun?"

"Get what?" Michael replies.

"Babe, I think that you're—"

"Don't!" Michael warns her, but she says it anyway.

"I think you're an ANGEL!"

"NO!" Michael protests.

"It's the only thing that makes sense."

"But it's physically impossible," Michael said as he touches his back feeling the feathers beneath his skin.

"I think when He is involved anything is possible."

"Who?" Michael replies.

"Babe, I am not a Christian nor a Catholic," Kelly says as she reaches for his hands to comfort him, "but even I know who could have done this. I think you just don't want to believe it."

Michael begins to shake his head, unwilling to hear the rest of what Kelly has to say.

"I mean think about it: you miraculously survived a lightning strike. He cured your cancer and now we find out you have wings! He definitely has something to do with this."

Michael stops shaking his head, then a tear begins to trickle from one of his eyes.

"Babe, what's wrong?" Kelly asks.

"I don't think I want it," Michael begins to weep in earnest

"Oh, Babe, why?" Kelly asks as she hugs her husband.

"A gift this great usually comes with a price," Michael tells her.

"The price can't be that great, considering he healed your cancer."

"I dunno," Michael mutters.

"Listen, I think we need to take a second here to address the elephant in the room," Kelly says, trying to lighten up the mood.

"What?"

"That God exists, and you're the proof! This is big! Don't you see?" Kelly places her hand under Michael's chin and raises her husband's lowered head. "God sent you back to us for a reason. For that I am grateful, no matter what the reason may be."

"You're right, Hun. You're right!" Michael agrees, wrapping his wife tightly into a hug and holding her that way for a long time, unaware that someone was lurking outside on the street pavement peering into the couple's window.

"We now have a chance," the stranger muttered to himself, then he smiled and walked off.

Chapter 8

The Affirmation

Michael slowly wakes up to the new morning and rubs his eyes, then he focuses on the television which is blaring a news report.

"What's going on?" he asks Kelly.

"It's all over the news," his wife replies, pointing to the screen. "It's as if the entire world has stood still."

"Hundreds of bodies have been pulled from the rubble since the fall of St Peter's Basilica," the female news reporter announces. *"The horse cloud that was surrounding the scene has disappeared, but in a disturbing development the Pope has been found dead in the Apostolic Palace of Vatican City—"*

"What!" Michael cries, sitting upright in his bed.

"I can't say how His Holiness died," the reporter continued grimly, *"but the detectives told me that it was the most gruesome crime scene they have ever witnessed. Those who are squeamish, please look away now."*

Written on the walls of the Pope's home in what looked suspiciously like blood was the following: *"We have killed your Leader; you are now leaderless in this WAR! Eden has fallen. Surrender!"*

"Oh my God!" Kelly cries hysterically. "Oh my God! Oh my God!"

"Babe, Babe, calm down," Michael says soothingly as he tries to hug his wife.

"They will find out who did this."

"NO!" Kelly says as she shoves him away. "I'm not scared of what has just happened! Don't you get it? You were miraculously healed from a traumatic event that you should have died in, then you were given wings! Don't you see what I am trying to say?"

Michael is dumbfounded. "No."

"This is why you were chosen, you dumbass!" she yells at her husband.

"What? No!" Michael replies, shaking his head.

"WAR!" Kelly cries, pointing at this word on the TV screen

Michael buries his head into his hands as he contemplates what this could all mean.

The reporter concludes, *"The authorities are asking that people everywhere remain calm and open minded, but vigilant during these uncertain times. We will keep you informed as this story develops."*

Kelly switches off the television and begins pacing the bedroom. "You are definitely not going to work today! If you ask why, I'm going to slap you!"

"It's Sunday," Michael reminds her.

Kelly stops pacing and yells at her husband. "AND?"

"Nothing!" Michael replies, then he gets out of bed and starts getting dressed.

"Where are you going?"

"To clear my head."

"Michael, the last time you cleared your head you got struck by lightning! You clear your head where I can see you."

"Can I at least go to the church?" he asks.

"Okay, I can deal with that," Kelly agrees, "it's not too far."

"Okay, I'm gonna head off," Michael says as he sprays himself with deodorant.

"I won't be long."

Michael kisses his wife and grabs his car keys, then he takes another look at Kelly. He can see how distraught she is, but she tries to smile for him as he leaves and heads to the garage.

"What does this all mean?" Michael mutters out loud to himself in the car, then as he begins to drive he looks up at the clouds through his windscreen. "Is this really why you chose me?"

He is hoping for an answer but, he doesn't get one. When he turns into the church parking lot he is surprised to find it empty. He parks his car and turns the ignition off, then he sees the priest exiting the church and beginning to lock up.

"Hey!" Michael yells out loud as he gets out of the car. "Hey, wait!"

"Sorry, the church is closed today," the priest says, trying to lock up quickly and be on his way. He is flustered and fumbles the keys as he begins to sniffle.

"Father, are you okay?" Michael asks as he places a hand on his shoulder.

"Yes." He sniffles some more then as he turns and sees Michael he exclaims in surprise, "You!"

"You remember me?"

"Yes, you were here before the storm. You were parked near the church and drove off in a rush."

"Yes, sorry that was me," Michael confesses. "I was also here another time. The guy with cancer who had lost his faith."

"Oh, yes, I do remember," the priest replied. "How's it all going?"

"Father…?"

"It's Father Brian."

"Father Brian, my name is Michael."

"Michael!" The priest smiles. "Good strong name!"

"Do you think we can speak inside?"

"Yes, of course," Father Brian says as he unlocks the doors. Michael enters the church and blesses himself with the holy water near the entrance.

Father Brian smiles. "I thought you'd lost your faith?"

"Yeah, well, things have changed, Father."

"Okay, that's good to know. Now, what seems to be troubling you?"

"Where do I begin?" Michael replies as he leans awkwardly against a church pew. "Um, you know that stuff that's happening on the TV?"

Father Brian bows his head. "Yes. It's the reason why I wanted to close up early today. I don't think I could have got through a sermon with all that going on,"

"With all due respect, Father, I think the people need it after all the terrible stuff that's happening."

"Hmm," Father Brian muses, then he looks up at Michael and said, "You're right; you're absolutely right. It's not about me. I will keep the doors open today." The priest smiles at Michael. "Thank you for that. Now what can I do for you?"

"Well, the night of the storm, I was struck by lightning."

"Oh!" Father Brian exclaimed. "So, you were one of those unfortunate ones?"

Michael is taken aback. "Wait, there were more people like me struck by lightning?"

The priest nodded. "Yes, there were quite a few. Some did not survive, so you were one of the lucky ones."

"I wouldn't say lucky," Michael replied dejectedly.

"What makes you say that?"

"Okay, don't freak out, Father," Michael warns him as he takes off his shirt.

"Uh, what's going on?" Father Brian says uncomfortably.

"Just wait!"

Michael tries to reach behind his back and reach into one of the slits to pull out a wing for he doesn't know how to make it come out willingly. He awkwardly pulls and pulls while Father Brian watches him in confusion.

Michael feels a sneezing sensation coming on. He blocks and it momentarily subsides, then he sneezes, and both his wings spread out. Spooked by this, Father Brian takes a tumble. He gazes up at Michael and sees him blocking the sunlight with both wings fully extended. Speechless, he blesses himself.

"Dear Lord!" he gasps as his jaw drops, then a feeling of complete peace comes over him.

"Are you okay?" Michael asks as he reaches down and offers Father Brian a hand. As he helps him to his feet, the priest begins to shed tears of joy.

"You are the answer, Michael! The answer to everyone's prayers!"

"No, I'm not," Michael retorts.

Father Brian smiles and places a hand on Michael's shoulder. "Don't you get it? On the same day we have lost a leader we have gained a GENERAL!"

"What do you mean a 'General'?"

"War was declared, and we were leaderless until you came along," Father Brian finishes with a smile

"No!" Michael cries, shaking his head. His wings retract back into his body as if in reaction to his disappointment.

"War is coming whether you like it or not," Father Brian told him, placing both hands on Michael's shoulders. "And there is no one better suited to lead us through this dark time than the General himself!"

"You keep saying 'General', why?"

"What is the name of the Angel that leads Gods army?"

"Wait, you think…you think, I am him?" Michael replies, stunned. "Why? Because I share his name?"

Father Brian responded with a nod.

"No, I am not the Archangel Michael!" he protests.

"God has work for you, Michael."

As Father Brian says these words, Michael recalls his computer screen at work telling him the same thing.

"He has chosen you because He sees something in you, something you may not yet see in yourself."

"I...I don't know where to go from here," Michael stammers. "I'm not a General! I'm not even a hero! He needs to take everything back; He made a mistake with me."

"No!" Father Brian replies firmly. "I make mistakes, you make mistakes, but HIM!" The priest points to the Heavens, "He never makes a mistake! NEVER!"

The congregation begins to enter the church and greet Father Brian, but the priest's gaze remains on Michael who panics and slowly backs up through the crowd.

"MICHAEL!" Father Brian yells as he pushes his way through the crowd and pursues him out of the church. Unfortunately, he's slowed down too much by his flock, and he gets out just in time to see Michael throw the car into gear and drive off.

Father Brian sighs and makes a small blessing before he heads back inside, whispering to himself, "I hope you find yourself soon, before it's too late for us all."

Chapter 9

Reunion

Kellys in the kitchen preparing breakfast for herself when she hears the garage doors opening.

"Oh, finally!" she mumbles to herself. She waits until she hears the inside garage door close before she demands, "well?"

Michael jumps, hardly expecting a welcome party in the kitchen. "Have you been waiting in here the whole time?"

"I'm just making myself breakfast. Well, is it good news or not?"

"It's definitely news…" Michael rubs his eyes, hardly believing what he has to report back to his wife. "I spoke with Father Brian and I told him everything."

"You told him you had wings?"

"Yeah, they kind of came out of me when I sneezed."

"What?" Kelly cries, startled. "Okay, we'll circle back to that. What did he say?"

"He thinks…" Michael pauses before muttering, "He thinks I'm an angel."

"I knew it!" Kelly yells as she slaps him on his shoulder.

"Oh, but not just any angel. He thinks I am *the* Angel Michael," he replies, spreading his hands out. Kelly stares at him. "There's an Angel named Michael?"

"Yes."

"And because you have the same name, he thinks you're him?"

"Yes!"

"What's so special about this Angel Michael?" Kelly asks. Well Michael in the Bible is the Archangel; the General of God's Army."

Kelly hits Michael in the arm again and shouts, "Oh my God! The General! The news said a War was coming, and now you have been chosen by God to be his General!"

Kelly hits Michael's arm again, much to his annoyance. "Stop doing that!" he says as he moves his arm away from his wife.

"Pfft! Some General!" Kelly jokes.

"And stop saying that!" Michael yells. "I'm *not* a General and I'm *not* fighting in a WAR!"

Kelly tries to be serious and sits them both down at the dining table. "Babe, you have a black belt in karate. You were an amateur Golden Gloves boxer as a teenager."

"Yes, but there's more to being a leader than knowing how to fight," Michael replies as he looks down at the table, "let alone a General—"

Kelly raises a hand in the air to silence his self-doubt. "You're a strategic thinker; you always think two steps ahead. When you plan, do or say something, you've already thought it through. If you ask me, I think the heavens have found their perfect General," Kelly concludes with a smile while Michael contemplates her words.

"You were always a sweet talker," Michael replies with a grin, then he kisses and embraces his wife.

"I learnt from the best," Kelly told him.

The couple's tender moment is interrupted by Michael's phone vibrating on the kitchen bench.

"Leave it!" Kelly pleads.

"Hang on, I just want to see who it is."

He picks up the phone and the screen tells him 'AMBROSE CALLING'.

"Shit!"

"What?"

"It's my brother," he responds

"So what?"

"It's Mum's Birthday." He checks the date on his phone and moans out loud. "YESTERDAY!"

"So, you missed a catch up with your brother? So what? You've been preoccupied with other important matters."

"This is Ambrose, Kelly; he won't understand."

"Exactly, so why worry about it if he doesn't care about your side of the story?"

"Cos he took it pretty hard when Mum passed. I'm all he has left."

"All I'm saying," Kelly says calmly as she cradles Michael's hand, "is that you've been through a lot as well. Ambrose needs to know that and to understand your side. Yes?"

"I make no promises," he says as he embraces her and kisses her on the forehead.

"You know he doesn't like me, right?"

"What? No!"

"Yeah, he thinks I split the family up," she quips half-jokingly.

"WHAT!"

"He does!" Kelly reiterates punching Michael playfully in the belly.

"I know, I know!" Michael laughs as he dodges her punch. "Don't let it get to you though. The more he holds onto a grudge, the more it eats him up."

"Yeah, but I feel bad you two are this way," she replies seriously. "You were as thick as thieves, now you barely see one another. The only day you see each other is on your Mum's birthday."

"Well, that's his fault, not yours. He knows my number if he wants to catch up."

"That goes both ways, love," Kelly reminds her husband. "I'm just saying," Kelly adds, shrugging her shoulders.

"Well, I better go and check in on him," Michael says as he kisses his wife's forehead again. "Bye!"

"Are you going to be back for lunch?" Kelly asks as Michael begins to leave the kitchen.

"Uh, maybe," Michael replies as he grabs his car keys. "I'll keep you posted."

***

At a quiet tavern a bartender cleans up tables and makes his way towards a patron.

"You finished with that?" he asks the man, nodding towards one of his empty glasses.

"Yes. And one more."

"Coming right up."

"What the hell's happening with the sports channel?" the man asks. "I'm missing the game!"

"The TV's been playing up all weekend," the bartender tries to explain, but when the man gives him a scowling look he promises, "I'll see what I can do."

Michael enters the tavern. His eyes dart around the room searching for someone. Finally they stop at the lonely, rude man at the table. Michael's shoulders slouch upon seeing him.

"Great!" he sighs, then he politely says out loud to the bartender. "Can I get a lemon, lime and bitters please?"

"Coming up!" the bartender acknowledges from behind the bar.

"Ambrose," Michael says with a nod as he approaches the table.

"You know this is a bar, right?"

"And...?" Michael prompts.

"Well, you're meant to get an alcoholic beverage, not a girl's drink!"

"I'm driving," Michael explains as he sits down at the table.

Ambrose downs half his drink in seconds, then there's a heavy silence between them both.

"Your lemon, lime and bitters, sir," the bartender says as he places the drink on the table before Michael.

"Thank you."

"God! You're such a boy scout!" Ambrose snorts, mocking his brother's manners. Michael ignores his attempt to start an argument and tries to shift the conversation.

"So, what's new with you?"

"Nothing." Ambrose says shortly.

"Come on, I'm sorry I missed her birthday, all right?" Michael apologises calmly, "I had—"

"I DON'T CARE WHAT YOU HAD ON!" Ambrose shouts back at Michael.

"THERE'S ALWAYS SOMETHING WITH YOU!"

"Is everything all right, gents?" the bartender asks with concern.

"Yep, we're good," Michael responds.

"Are we?" Ambrose mutters.

"I know you're not going to believe me, but something happened to me—"

"Nope," Ambrose interjects then he abruptly leaves the table. Michael follows him as he exits the tavern.

"Wait! Will you stop and listen?"

When Michael places a hand on Ambrose's shoulder to stop him he punches Michael across the left side of his face. Michael retaliates in kind but immediately feels guilty when Ambrose spits some blood out onto the pavement.

"I'm sorry, Ambrose."

"I knew you had it in you!" he growls, then he heads for his car.

"WAIT!" Michael yells, but Ambrose has already jumped into his car and is leaving the parking lot.

Michael draws in a deep breath, then loudly exhales. "Great!" he murmurs to himself.

Chapter 10

Answers

The cardinals begin to gather at the Church of Saint Michael and Magnus, near the rubble of St Peter's Basilica in Vatican City. Normally there are over two hundred cardinals, however this gathering consists of a mere twenty.

"Is this all we have?" one cardinal asks, surprised.

"The other cardinals are afraid to set foot on these grounds where His Holiness recently died," Cardinal Joseph, the Dean of the College of Cardinals, responds. "They are afraid that's all; do not judge them."

"Why are we gathering anyway?" the disgruntled cardinal asks, "it is too soon to choose a successor."

"We are here to discuss other important matters."

"What other important matters?"

"Show them, Cardinal Joseph!" Cardinal Vincent, the vice-dean, suggests.

"Show us what?"

"This!" Cardinal Joseph says as he hands around photos. "This has been held back from the press at our request."

"What is this?" one asks with a frown.

"Claw marks over a meter long," Cardinal Joseph replies grimly. "We think this is the work of the Devil."

Every cardinal laughs until Cardinal Joseph throws down the last photo.

"Here!"

The cardinals all gasp in horror as the picture shows the Pope's headless body with a message cut into his bare chest saying, "We are already here!"

They all blessed themselves and recited the 'Hail Mary' then one cardinal asks, "What does this mean?"

"That is what we are here to discuss," Cardinal Joseph replies. "First, we need to send messages to every archbishop and bishop. They must know the truth, and what potentially is to come."

"And what exactly is coming?"

Cardinal Joseph looks around and sees he now has everyone's full attention. "I honestly don't know. This has never happened before."

"What do you personally think is happening, Cardinal Joseph?" one asks cautiously.

"I believe this is a proclamation of war."

"Can we stop them?" a terrified cardinal asks.

Cardinal Joseph shrugs his shoulders. "We are but men. If these perpetrators are what we think they are, then we have no hope of stopping them."

A few of the cardinals look at one another.

"We must have faith in—" Cardinal Joseph is interrupted by some of the cardinals leaving.

"Where are you going?" Cardinal Vincent calls, rising to his feet.

"Let them go!" Cardinal Joseph tells him. "They are scared, and I cannot blame them."

The vice-dean sits back down. Cardinal Joseph takes in a big breath and sighs. "Their faith has been tested and so has mine, but I will stay faithful. I trust in Him and He will not forsake us!"

Despite the dean's confident proclamation, the remaining cardinals are worried.

***

As Michael drives back home from the tavern, he looks in his rear-view mirror and sees a cut on his lip from his brother's punch. He wipes the blood off using the collar of his shirt but more blood trickles out.

"Damn it!"

When he turns down his street, he sees a stranger standing on the walkway outside his place. He turns into his driveway but doesn't open the garage just yet.

"Can I help you?" Michael asks as he exits his car.

"I was just admiring your house," the stranger replies as he turns away with the sun setting behind him. "It looks cosy."

"Do I know you?" Michael asks warily. "You seem familiar."

"I must have a familiar face."

"Well, I wouldn't know since you're facing away from me."

The stranger turns around and begins, "Okay, don't freak out—"

"YOU!" Michael shouts as he recognises the stranger from the train station. He walks over to him, but the stranger waves his hands telling him to dial down his tone.

"SHH!"

"I don't know how, but I know you have something to do with this!"

"With what?"

"Don't play dumb! You know!"

"Oh, you mean the wings, the strength, the impenetrable body—"

"WHAT?" Michael interrupts. "No, I only have wings!"

"You're sure only wings?"

"Yes, I'm sure," Michael responds as he points to his split lip.

"Huh!" The stranger inspects him and asks, "What happened here?"

"My pissed off brother happened."

"No! That shouldn't be," the stranger says, puzzled. "Here," he places a hand over the cut, and it heals instantly. "There you go, all better!" he declares as he removes his hand.

"What?" Michael feels the side of his face to discover his cut is healed and the pain has gone. "YOU!" he cries as he takes a step back. "You… you're Him? So, you did give me my wings?"

"And everything else that comes with it. You just haven't explored them yet."

"Why me?"

"Why not you?"

"Because I'm old!" Michael protests. "And this is a young man's game. I have a family to protect; I can't be risking my life."

"Ah, but you're wrong. That is what makes you the perfect candidate. Your best quality as a human being is your protective nature. You get this from being the eldest brother in the family and being a father. You looked after your four younger brothers when your parents were out working, you fed them and took them to school. You also took the blame for them when they destroyed something in the house—a window, the television. You were disciplined again and again by your parents for this."

Michael swallows a lump in his throat and stands stoic as the stranger recites his life story.

"Now you're a father of three children. You watch your kids sleep for ten minutes before going to bed yourself because you like to see them at peace."

Michael's resolve is crumbling and he feels a single tear roll down his cheek. The stranger places both his hands on Michael's broad shoulders and continues, "And now, when your own kids are being destructive or cheeky, not once have you raised your hand to discipline them." The stranger smiles at Michael. "It is your temperament that sold me on you. Most people would love to have this power. A parent's instinct is to protect, and you have that written all over you. Am I wrong?"

Michael thinks for a moment, then as he raises his head he knows his life is going to change. "No." he finally answers.

"I'm sorry to burden you with this gift, but I feel that there was no one else better suited for what's to come."

The outside veranda light turns on, then Kelly shouts, "Who's out there?"

"Just me, Hun! I'm coming in now," Michael calls, turning towards the house. He turns back to where the stranger was, "…sorry, you were saying something is coming?" But when he finishes, he realises the stranger, as always, has disappeared.

Chapter 11

Moment of Truth

Kelly's preparing dinner for everyone as Michael enters their home and is greeted by his family.

"Hey, Dad!" both boys yell from the dining table.

"Hey, boys," Michael responds, then he yells to his daughter locked up in her room, "Hey Em!"

Her response is heard faintly in the kitchen. "Hey!"

Kelly asks her husband, "Who were you talking to outside?"

"Oh, just the neighbour," he responds quickly.

"What did he want?"

"Just wishing us all a Merry Christmas," Michael replies, surprised at how quick he came up with the lie.

"Are we all sorted for Christmas?" Kelly asks. "It's a day away from Christmas Eve."

"I don't know. I've been preoccupied for two weeks."

"Get out of here! Kelly says, whacking him playfully with the tea towel.

"Was there anything more on the news about…?" Michael trails off and looks at the boys to make sure they're not listening. "That stuff about the Vatican City?"

"Nothing I've heard."

"Hmm, okay," Michael replies, then he hears sirens blaring outside.

"That sounds pretty close," Kelly says to Michael. "Quick, turn the TV on!"

He rushes for the remote and switches on the television.

"Breaking news!" the news reporter announces. *"There has been an explosion in a townhouse believed to be a drug lab in the Northern Suburb of Midland."*

"What!" Kelly rushes over to get a closer look at the screen. "That's a suburb over from us."

"Some of the debris from the explosion landed on neighbouring houses which caught alight very quickly."

Kelly turns to her husband. "You should go!"

"What?" Michael replies.

"You know, so no one gets hurt."

"Emergency services are believed to be on their way…"

"There! You see, its being handled," Michael tells Kelly as he points to the screen.

"However, from our view from the helicopter we can see men who do appear to be armed and wearing masks, and it looks as though they are heading towards the neighbouring home…"

"Oh my God!" Kelly shouts. "You have got to go now!"

Kelly turns to face her husband, but Michael is nowhere to be seen.

"Michael?"

Kelly goes looking for her husband. She hears the garage door opening and looks out the front door to see his car reversing and speeding off down the street. She runs back to the television to see everything unfold. The boys sitting at the dining table are baffled by their mother's behaviour.

"Mum, are you okay?" Hudson asks.

"I'm okay, Hun. Just eat your dinner. There's something on the TV that is important to Mummy."

"Can I see?"

"No, not yet, Hun," Kelly answers swiftly. "I'll come and get you when you can see, okay?"

Disappointed Hudson turns his head away. "Yes, Mum"

Michael speeds down the nearly empty highway to Midland and spots the news helicopter in the air. He follows it and ten minutes later sees the smoke rising from the burning houses.

"Bingo!" he whispers to himself. He tries to find a secluded spot to hide his car and parks one street over from the destroyed homes, near a park. He hops out of his car and runs as fast as he can towards the burning homes.

As he nears the scene Michael can overhear the exchange between the cops and the suspects, somewhere between threats and negotiations. He creeps along and then hides himself in nearby thick shrubs. Fortunately, the neighbouring home is the last house on the street and near the park. In the darkness no one is aware of his presence as he looks on and bides his time, waiting to be useful.

At home, Kelly clings to every word from the news reporter.

"The fire department has arrived at the scene, but the hostage situation unfolding at the front of the house makes their task more difficult."

From his position, Michael can hear everything, every quiver in the young cops voice. "Take it easy!" the police constable is calling to one of the armed men.. "We need you to lower the gun. Nobody needs to get hurt here!"

"What do I do? what do I do?" Michael mutters to himself as he watches everything unfold.

"DROP YOUR GUNS!" the hostage taker yells at the police in a threatening manner, pressing his nine-millimetre gun harder into the lady's throat. "DROP EM NOW!"

"Okay, easy!" Both police officers hold their hands up in the air, then they slowly lower their guns and place them on the ground.

"Okay, now will you let her go?" one of the officers asks.

The criminals inch towards the first home, then suddenly a car ignition turns on.

"Quick, into the car!" one thug yells to the other as he pushes the terrified hostage into the getaway car.

Both police officers dive for their guns as the offenders begin firing at them.

"Go! Go! Go!" the thug with the hostage yells at the getaway driver, while his accomplice is still shooting at the police.

The police and fire fighters hide behind their vehicles as the car drives off, still shooting wildly. A wayward bullet narrowly misses Michael.

"Shit!" he says as he hides himself fully behind the tree, then he hears a girl screaming from inside one of burning houses.

Michael instinctively runs towards the scream, ignoring the shoot-out that is currently happening as the police return fire. As the thug's car drives away from the crime scene, the news helicopter gives chase trying to assist the Police Department.

"No, No, No!" Kelly screams at the TV, wanting the news reporters to stay on scene where Michael could be.

No one sees Michael running towards the building which is almost engulfed in flames. He enters the home and calls loudly, "Hello? Hello?"

Coughing, Michael continues walking down the corridor. "Where are you?" he whispers to himself. He sees a trail of blood on the floor, suggesting someone is around the corner in the kitchen. He follows it and finds a little girl panting rapidly and holding onto her stomach.

"Hey, hey, hey!" Michael races towards her. "I'm here, I'm here!"

She struggles to speak. "Something hit my belly...really hard!" she manages to get out, then she begins to cough up blood.

"Shh, shh!" Michael soothes, then he grabs hold of her hands to peek at the wound.

"Damn it!" he says when he sees it's a gunshot wound. When he applies pressure to it she screams.

"I'm sorry, I'm sorry," Michael apologises. "It's supposed to help. What's your name?"

"Cha—Charlotte."

"Okay, Charlotte, I need to get you outside."

"Okay," she says quietly.

"Up we go!" Michael says as he picks her up and cradles her gently in his arms. Suddenly the ceiling fails and caves inwards.

"Shit!"

Michael embraces Charlotte, using his body to shield her from the debris and flames the best he can. In this moment of selflessness, his wings react and eject outwards, shielding them both.

The fire and ambulance services are still on scene. As the fire fighters begin to prep their equipment they hear the crackling of the burning houses, then they take cover as one house begins to collapse.

The ash and wood debris falls off Michael's wings as he begins to walk towards the emergency personnel. Their jaws drop in awe as they witness the miraculous rescuer that is approaching them. Michael can now control his wings at will, so he spreads them out and gives them a shake to get rid of any debris that maybe clinging to it.

Charlotte opens her eyes and sees a blurred vision of Michael with his wings out protecting her. "Are you my guardian angel?"

Michael is lost for words. His face is filled with sadness, for he can see her life drifting in and out every time she blinks. He says the one thing that may be comforting to her.

"Yes, my name is Michael," he says as he presses against her wound, fully accepting the gift that has been bestowed upon him. He feels a subtle warm sensation emitting from under his hand as he carries Charlotte, but he thinks nothing of it. He approaches one of the ambulance officers who is a little daunted to be in Michael's presence. She reaches out her quivering arms to receive Charlotte.

"She's been shot in the stomach," Michael tells the medic. "It looks like a clean shot, straight through."

Charlotte's body gave out the moment she was handed over. The ambulance officer places the girl on the stretcher and begins CPR. Shocked by this, Michael takes a few steps backwards and watches them trying to revive Charlotte.

Rage sets in and boils to the surface. Michael raises both his arms into the air and bends his knees slightly as if he was going to dive into the sky from a vertical jump. As he raises his arms his wings do the same, then he drops them downwards. This action propels him high up into the air. Using the helicopter's location as a guide, he flies towards the thugs at top speed.

"Shoot at the helicopter!" the getaway driver calls to his sidekick, noting that the police are in hot pursuit, "They're giving away our location!"

"PISS OFF!" one of the thug's shouts while shooting at the helicopter. The aircraft backs away and keeps its distance.

"Please let me go," the hostage pleads tearfully. "I have a daughter."

"QUIET!"

They begin to shoot at the police car and manage to take out a tyre, causing the car to lose control. The police car crashes into a bollard on the side of the highway; both officers exit the vehicle unharmed but disorientated.

Michael takes advantage. While no one is looking he lands in front of the thug's car, allowing the vehicle to crash into him. Everyone inside the car is thrown about, for no one was wearing a seatbelt, including the hostage. The driver is worse for wear, but the other two thugs regain their composure pretty quickly.

"What the hell happened?"

They look at each other, then they see Michael standing in front of their car, radiating fury. As he makes his way towards the passenger door, one of the thugs yells to the other, "Shoot him, shoot him!"

Michael rips open the car door and reaches for the closest thug, whose gun is now empty. He grabs hold of him and tosses him to the side of the road. The other criminal fires his two remaining bullets at Michael but they have no effect when they pelt against his body.

Michael opens the rear door grabs hold of the thug's leg and tosses him aside where he lands on his unconscious buddy and is knocked out cold.

Having disposed of the criminals, Michael turns his attention towards the hostage. The poor lady is cringing on the floor, shaking in fear and shielding her head from any danger.

"Are you okay?" Michael asks gently.

She takes some time to gather her wits. Lowering her hands, she looks at Michael and asks, "What…who are you?"

"Take my hand. Your daughter needs you," Michael says quickly, for he hears the helicopter coming back.

"Is she okay?" she asks as she reaches for Michael's hand.

Unable to lie to her, he replies, "She's hurt."

"Can you take me to her?"

Michael is unsure. He acted out of rage and his wings instinctively did the rest. Now he is calmer doubt fills him. "I can try," he replies as he picks her up in his arms.

"You have wings," she points out to Michael. "I saw you fly."

"Yes, but I'm still new to all of this. When I flew I was angry. I just knew what I wanted to do and did it."

She tries to help him. "Well, think back and remember the moment it happened."

"I wanted to get to you and not let these thugs get away. All I saw was red."

"It seems you acted on emotion. Anger can be a strong emotion, but Love is stronger, and you need to get a mother back to her scared daughter."

"Right." Michael smiles but remembers that her daughter was shot and is in a critical condition. As his emotion begins to take over he feels his wings reacting to him, like a muscle twitching on command. He spreads his wings and clings on to the mother, then as his wings propel downward he shoots up into the air. To try and remain unseen, Michael flies high above the helicopter and asks his passenger a question.

"What's your name?"

"Huh?"

"Your name. What is it?"

"It's Hayley," she responds, looking up at him.

"Hayley, I'm Michael," he says with a smile, then he looks for a discreet spot to land near what remains of her house. He chooses the nature reserve nearby.

"Are you supposed to tell me your name?"

"I trust you," he says as he lands gently on the ground and releases her.

"Okay, now your daughter was in pretty bad shape when I left her with the ambulance," Michael warns her as his wings retract back into his body.

"What happened?" Hayley asks as they both run towards the ambulance.

Michael is unsure how to break the news to Hayley. Upon seeing Charlotte lying motionless on the stretcher he fears the worst.

"She's okay." the ambulance offer informs them, then she says to Michael, "I thought you said she was shot?"

"She was," Michael replies, then seeing her name tag he adds, "Lucy, she was shot in the belly."

"There was a lot of blood where you say she was shot, but no bullet wound," Lucy replies, showing Charlotte's belly to both Michael and Hayley. There's no sign of any wound.

Michael looks at his hand. *Did I heal her?* "So, is she going to be okay?"

"Yes," Lucy confirms.

"That's great!" Michael replies with a big dorky grin on his face, then he briefly hugs Hayley to celebrate.

Still caught off guard by it all, Hayley points to her daughter and asks, "So, is she…"

"She'll be fine," Lucy assures her. "She's just resting. She's been through a lot."

Hearing more sirens making their way towards their location, Michael says in a stern voice, "Right, I best be off. Can I count on you two to keep this under wraps for now, especially my identity?"

"Uh, sure," Hayley replies. "It's the least I can do for saving my life and taking care of Charlotte."

"Definitely!" Lucy adds.

"Really?" Michael replies, surprised they're both willing to comply.

"Yeah, I mean when an angel asks you to do to something, you do it" Lucy says. "Honestly, it's nice to know that you're out there."

"Thank you," Michael says smiling graciously at them both, then he returns to the nature reserve and disappeared into the darkness.

"BYE!" Lucy and Hayley shout out, hoping Michael will hear them.

The fire fighters almost have the blaze under control and more police officers arrive on scene.

Meanwhile, Michael is trying to locate his car. "Come on, come on!" he mutters. "Where did I leave you? Ah, that's it!" he says as he unbuttons his side pocket of his cargo pants and pulls out the keyless fob. He pushes the button and can faintly hear the car beeping.

"A-ha!" he says as he runs towards the noise. He presses it again and this time sees his car beep as the headlights flicker.

"There you are!"

Michael jogs faster towards his car. He unlocks it and clambers inside quickly before the helicopter hovers over his location. With a big sigh of relief, he allows his adrenaline to subside. "Wow, what a night!"

Chapter 12

Accipio

Kelly watches the television intently, hoping for news updates.

"The authorities appear to have the situation under control," the reporter says. *"It looked as though the criminals were going to get away with a hostage, but the police have apprehended them, and the hostage is now safe and with her daughter."*

Kelly smiles at the TV. "Was that you, Babe?" she wonders aloud, then hearing the

garage door opening she runs from the lounge and opens the door leading from their kitchen into the garage.

"Soooo!" she says from doorway as Michael opens his car door. "Did it go okay?"

"Yeah, I think it went well," Michael smiles as he makes his way to his wife and gives her a kiss.

"Come, the news is still on!" Kelly says as he closes the garage, then she clings tightly to Michael's hand as she leads him into the lounge.

"Ooh, look they're interviewing people now. Do you know them?" Kelly asks as she points at the lady on the screen.

"Yes, that's Hayley. She's the hostage and the mother of the girl I helped."

"Oh, how exciting!" Kelly replied, grinning from ear to ear. "Um, is she going to keep your secret? She is on national TV."

"Of course! We have a deal," Michael tells his wife while the news reporter continues to speak with Hayley.

"So, what can you tell us about your ordeal?"

"It was scary at first, being taken as hostage and away from my daughter, but when he came along I knew I was safe."

"The police you mean, ma'am?"

"No, my guardian angel. He was the real hero. When he showed up and tossed those thugs aside all my fears went away."

Kelly stops watching the TV and observes her husband soaking in the glory. She smiles, happy for him to have this moment.

"Does this hero have a name?" the news reporter asks.

"No, but he has wings," Hayley replies with a smile. In the background Lucy the ambulance officer can be seen slapping her forehead in frustration.

"DAMN IT, MICHAEL!" Kelly yells.

"What? She didn't tell everyone my name, at least."

"Oh, give her time and she will!" Kelly shouts.

"Well, I trust her," Michael replies, then he asks, "Where are the kids?"

"It's late. They're all in bed."

"Okay, well I'm going to have a shower and then I might think about going to bed too," Michael tells Kelly.

"Yeah, me too," Kelly replies, then as they both head off to their bedroom she adds teasingly, "Guardian Angel!"

***

In the VIP area of a nightclub, a powder in a sealable pouch is passed around by a police constable.

"That's twenty dollars a bag," Peter Dolan tells the guy accepting it.

"Okay," he replies as he rises from his bean bag and reaches for his wallet. As he does so, Constable Dolan looks over across the bar and spots his offsider, Constable Sacks. The two nod at each other, then she continues to negotiate her deal.

"Here you go," the buyer says as he hands the money to Constable Dolan.

"Remember, before you snort the drug you must say 'Accipio', otherwise the drug won't be as effective."

"Huh, weird," the guy mutters.

"Accipio, means 'I accept' in Latin,'" Peter explains. "That's why the drug is called 'Accipio'."

"Okay." The buyer places some powder on the web region between his thumb and index finger.

"Accipio," he says and nods to Peter, then he snorts the powder and is immediately affected. His eyes flicker and then glow orange-red, then he has a dramatic seizure which last for twenty seconds. His whole-body droops, much to the horror of onlookers who think he has just died. Suddenly, he gasps frantically for air as if new life has just been given to him. His eyes remain orangey red and he looks up at Constable Dolan. They share a smile, then the guy draws in a big breath and exhales deeply as if in enjoyment.

Those who witnessed this event are impressed, the low-life dry culture alive and well.

"Give me one! I'll take some!" they all yell at Peter.

He grins and winks across the bar at Sacks. "Don't worry, there's plenty to go around!"

Chapter 13

The Strength Within

A mobile phone rings, echoing throughout the empty church. The priest answers it. "Hello, Father Brian speaking." He listens for a while then he asks, "Have the other Dioceses been contacted? Yes, thank you, we'll be on high alert here."

Michael walks into the church and seeing no one else calls out loud, "Hello?"

Father Brian holds his hand up to Michael to appeal for quiet as he is still on the phone. Michael nods and sits in one of the church pews to wait for him.

"Yes, there is one more thing. I wish to speak with the Dean of the College of Cardinals; I have some news which will be of interest to him. Tell His Eminence this may turn the tide for us," Father Brian concludes as he watches Michael. "Yes, the cardinal can contact me anytime on this number. Okay, thank you, goodbye."

Father Brian hangs up, then he draws in a deep breath, mindlessly fingers his dog collar and approaches Michael,

"I'm surprised to see you again. I thought I'd scared you off!" he jokes.

"Oh, no, sorry," Michael apologises. "It was just a lot to take in, especially coming from you."

"Well I'm sorry I upset you that day" Father Brian says as he sits beside Michael. "That wasn't my intention."

After an awkward silence, the priest prompts, "So, what's brought you here today?"

"Oh, right. I'm not sure if you have had a chance to see the news, Father."

Father Brian smiles. "Yes, I have. Was that you?"

"Yes," Michael almost whisper, looking down at the floor

"Is this good or bad?" Father Brian asks as he studies his body language. "Because you're hard to read."

"Sorry, I'm just reflecting on the event," he says as he stands up, beginning to pace.

"Are you okay?" Father Brian asks Michael, watching him with interest..

"I flew."

"What?" Father Brian gasps as he releases Michael

"I flew," he repeats while the priest sits back down on the pew and tries to process what Michael has just said. "I think I can control my wings now."

Father Brian remains silent,

"Well?" Michael prompts.

"Sorry, it's just hit me," he said as he stands again.

"What has just hit you?"

Father Brian's mind begins to race. "You're real. You're going to change A LOT of lives. Not just by saving them. The first moment they set their eyes on you, their lives will change instantly. I know because that moment has already happened to me."

"What moment, Father?" Michael asks curiously.

"THAT GOD EXISTS!" he exclaims to Michael. They stare at each other for a moment until the phone rings.

"Do you need to get that?" Michael asks.

"It can go to voicemail," Father Brian replies.

"It may be someone important."

"I don't have anyone of importance contacting me over the festive holidays," Father Brian responds then he belatedly remembers he had asked to speak with the dean.

"OH, SUGAR!" he shouts as he runs out the door. "Don't you leave, Michael!"

He misses the call, then he quickly runs back to Michael to ensure he hasn't left.

"What?" Michael asks, raising his hands in the air and smirking. "Don't you trust me?"

"Well, you have a bad habit of leaving," Father Brian replies

"Well, I'm here now. And I think you're going to get a kick out of what I have to say next," Michael says with a smile.

"What is it?" Father Brian asks curiously.

"You may want to sit down for this, Father"

"Is it bad?" he asks as he follows his suggestion.

"No, I don't believe so," Michael mutters under his breath. "I, um… I spoke with Him."

"You spoke with who?" Father Brian asks.

"With HIM!" Michael says in a sterner manner looking up to the heavens.

"What?!!" Father Brian cries, then he stands up and places a hand over his mouth. "When? How? What did you speak about?"

"Last night we spoke, face-to-face" Michael explains. "He was outside my house, so I confronted Him."

"YOU WHAT!" Father Brian yells at Michael.

"Well, I thought he was a stalker," Michael responds.

"Sweet God!" the priest breathes.

"Can you actually say that?" Michael asks.

"Don't start!" Father Brian warns, then he asks, "Well, what did you speak about?"

"He told me about my life, and how it had all led to this point," Michael replies as he stands up and leans against a church pew, "He really does see everything!"

"He is God!" Father Brian reminds him, then out of curiosity he asks, "So… what did He look like?"

"He was dressed as a homeless guy," Michael replied with a smile.

"Uh-huh," the priest muttered under his breath. "Well, that makes sense, don't you think?"

"What?"

"How else can you go undetected?" Father Brian told him. "Who would you notice more: a high profile, arrogant rich man or someone that people don't give a second thought about. He even fooled you, and you're an angel!!"

Father Brian laughs, enjoying his dig at Michael. The two stand together enjoying each other's company before the priest clears his throat and begins awkwardly, "I have something to ask."

"What is it?" Michael asks.

"Earlier when the phone rang, I was actually expecting someone important to call," Father Brian began in a slow manner, unsure of what Michael's response would be. "I am expecting a call from Cardinal Joseph. He is the Dean of the College of Cardinals, second only to the Pope himself."

"Okay," Michael says.

"Well, I was hoping with your permission I could tell him about you."

Spooked by this, Michael turns his back on Father Brian.

"Please, Michael. They're looking for answers right now," Father Brian pleads, choosing his words carefully. "Knowing of your existence will put a lot of people at ease and lift their spirits, as it did mine."

"I…I don't think I'm ready," Michael says gently, but he can see the disappointment on the priest's face. He begins to walk backwards.

"Where are you going?" Father Brian asks.

"I'm sorry, I can't. I'm not ready yet," Michael says as he leaves the church.

Undeterred, the priest chases after him and this time catches up to Michael. "You can't run from this!" he says, placing a hand on his shoulder and turning him around to face him. "This responsibility has been bestowed upon you by the highest power."

"I know, but…"

"But what?" Father Brian interrupts Michael.

"As soon as I accept that responsibility, it becomes real!" Michael adds. "The normal life I have will be over and my family will have to be set aside."

Father Brian empathises with Michael. "I see it now. Your strength comes from your family. It's both overwhelming and unpredictable."

"What does that mean, Father?'

"It means your strength is limitless. I don't think even God knows the extent of your strength and nor do you."

"How will I know when I am ready?"

"You don't," the priest replied, "that moment finds you. We have a saying for that."

"What is it?" Michael asks

Father Brian's smile is wry. "Baptism by fire."

Chapter 14

Baptism By Fire

A demonic horde gathers beneath a busy freeway and grows exponentially. Growls are heard from the horde as some clash against each other as there is nearly no room left under the bridge. Some stand still in a trance like state, possibly the ones that have been there the longest. The new ones are still rowdy. They cannot leave the bridge location, no matter how large the horde. Are they waiting for something, or are they afraid to leave?

A bus parks at the end of the bridge tunnel, blocking it so no one else can come through.

"I have new recruits," Constable Peter Dolan announces as he exits the bus.

"Good!" A huge, disfigured figure rises from the back of the horde, its eyes a gruesome red colour. "Though we're nearly at maximum capacity. I did not realise how easily corruptible human souls are," he says with a terrifying laugh. "At this rate this war will be over before it begins."

He laughs again and Peter joins in.

The creature grabs hold of a random person, one of his possessed soldiers. . "Hold still!" he says as he places him over a seal which then emits light. The creature mutters in a demon dialect, then blue flames emerge and incinerates the possessed person instantly.

As Peter begins to package up the powder left behind, a flock of frightened ducks fly through the tunnel under the bridge. He dodges the ducks but accidently bumps the creature as he was hunched over. Peter fumbles the powder which flies into the air and is accidentally inhaled by the ducks. Their adrenaline skyrockets from the powder. After they exit the tunnel, they shoot high up into the sky and circle each other as if trying to be rid of this new energy burst.

A passing airplane sucks the ducks into its left engine which malfunctions and emits dark smoke and a loud bang.

"YOU!" the angry creature cries, grabbing Constable Dolan by the throat. "That was our last batch and you drew attention to us!"

"I didn't know!" Peter winces as his throat is slowly being crushed, "I'm sorry!"

"You can be the final batch," the creature mutters.

"No! I am a match with this human!" he protests, but these are his final last words. The creature breaks his neck, drops his lifeless body on the seal and begins the ritual again.

"Take this last batch and bring me back more soldiers!" the creature says to Constable Megan Sacks.

"I won't fail you," she says as she accepts the bag of powder.

"Good. If you do fail me…" The creature points to the bag of powder to explain Megan's fate if she fails, then he shoos her away saying, "GO!"

***

Michael parks outside a local florist to collect some flowers he'd ordered for Kelly. Unfortunately for him, there was a news crew outside the shop doing a report on how busy the local florist had been over the Christmas holidays. Michael manoeuvres behind the cameraman trying to stay out of view, then he speaks to the young lady behind the counter.

"Hi, I am picking up some flowers."

"Yep, what was the name?" she asks.

"Uh, under Michael," he responds.

"Ok, yep, we have them here. That will be forty dollars," she says as she gets the till ready.

"Here you go," Michael hands her a fifty and says, "Keep the change."

"Thank you and Merry Christmas!"

"Merry Christmas!" he replies with a wave as he leaves.

Suddenly, everyone ducks for cover as they hear a loud bang coming from the sky.

Michael looks up and sees a airplane with one of its engines on fire and the sky filled with dark smoke. The cameraman points his camera into the air getting a full view of the damaged plane while the news reporter flips their script and begins an ad hoc report on the developing story.

Michael recalled his conversation with Father Brian: *That moment finds you!'*

He rushes to his car and places his flowers gently on the passenger seat, then he starts the vehicle and heads in the direction where the plane was going down.

On board the stricken plane, everyone is flustered and panicked. Screams from both adults and children can be heard in the cockpit. "Everyone please have your seat belts on and ensure you're in the brace position," the pilot says over the intercom. Both he and his co-pilot are doing what they can to keep the plane steady, but the engine now blows on the left side of the plane, causing the plane to spin.

Meanwhile, Michael drives as best he can to catch the plane but is slowed down by onlookers who have stopped on the road and are watching the plane as it dives.

"What are you all doing?" he whispers to himself as he looks at everyone gawking at the plane. Blocked, he has no choice but to pull his car off to the side of the road. He gets out and thinks for a moment. *What to do, what to do? It's daytime which means my identity can be seen.*

"Fudge it!" he says aloud as he ejects his wings, ripping away his shirt. He raises his wings and jets himself into the air. A gust of wind created from his wings propels him into the air higher and higher. People on the ground look around to see what is happening, but thanks to Michael's swiftness all they see is a speck streaking towards the plane.

"Look!" the onlookers cry as they all point towards him. "What is that?"

"This is crazy! This is crazy!" Michael mutters under his breath.

"Boeing 777 you have an unidentified object coming up on your port side," ground control informs the pilot and co-pilot. They both look over to see what it is, but nothing seems to be there

.

Back at the local church presbytery, Father Brian returns the call he missed earlier today.

"Cardinal Joseph's office," a lady from administration answers. "How may I help you?"

"My name is Father Brian and I'm returning a call from His Eminence,"

"I will put you through now, Father," she replies. While he waits, Father Brian notices the live news on his television showing an airplane on fire.

"WHAT!"

"Hello, Father Brian," Cardinal Joseph says politely as he answers the phone, but there is no response. "Father Brian, are you there?"

"Yes, I am here, Your Eminence," he replies but his attention is still fixed on the television.

"I hope you are aware that the Pope's passing was suspicious in nature," the cardinal says, but again he gets no reply. "Hello? Am I keeping you from something, Father Brian?"

"No, no, sorry, Cardinal Joseph."

"You said you had something to tell me," the cardinal reminds him, "Something that may turn the tide of the events that have unfolded?"

"Yes, Your Eminence."

"Well? What is it?"

"Turn your television on, Cardinal Joseph."

"I live in ROME! Your Australian news won't be available to me here!"

"Our local news is about to go global," Father Brian says.

"What!?"

"Come on, Michael, this is your moment," Father Brian whispers.

As Michael flies closer and closer to the plane, he watches the aircraft carefully trying to judge when to act as it spins out of control.

"Oh my God!" cries one of the reporters witnessing the event. Regrettably her cameraman has yet to set himself up to report the news. "There is someone flying alongside the plane! Quickly, quickly!" she yells at her cameraman.

"Okay," Michael says as he straightens both his wings out to glide and waits for the destroyed port engine to spin around once more. "Okay, NOW!" he shouts to himself, then he catches the wing before it spirals again. His right arm clings tightly to the plane's wing. Using every ounce of his strength to ensure the plane does not spiral again, he uses his right wing to whack the damaged engine, trying to detach it.

"One. . .!" Michael counts as he gives the engine a whack. "Come on, two!"

He gets frustrated as the engine still does not budge. He takes in a deep sigh, hoping the last strike will have some effect.

"THREE!"

His wing smacks hard against the damaged engine. This time it detaches and drops into a nearby lake, avoiding further catastrophe. Michael is now able to hold the wing upright with both hands without the dead weight of a destroyed engine, he grips the wing tightly ensuring the plane does not spiral again. His wings glide through the air, keeping the plane steady and flap as needed if the plane begins to spiral.

"What you are about to see is footage that is not edited, it is coming to you LIVE!" the news reporter says as the cameraman zooms up close to the damaged plane with Michael alongside it. *"It appears to be a real live angel coming to the rescue of this passenger plane."*

"We are now stable," the relieved co-pilot tells the pilot, then he glances outside the port window of the cockpit and sees Michael holding the wing. "Uh, Captain, there's someone out there holding the port wing."

"What?!"

"I'm not kidding!" he replies, then the pilot takes a look.

"Be cool, Michael, be cool!" he thinks to himself as he sees the pilot gawking at him.

"Mama, look!" a little girl taps her mother on the shoulder and points towards her window on the plane.

"Baby, you have to sit in brace position like everyone else is," she says to her distracted daughter.

"Whoa! What is that?" other people exclaim when they see Michael through their own windows.

Seeing that everyone is now looking through their windows, the mother takes a peep and brushes her daughter back to get a clear view.

"My goodness!" she says out loud when she sees a man with silvery feathered wings spread out wide in the sunlight.

"Is he an angel, Mommy?" the little girl asks her mother.

"I don't know, Hun!" she replies with a smile, "but I hope so."

"Okay, now brace for landing, Michael!" he tells himself as the ground begins to get closer and closer.

"Everyone please brace yourselves as we prepare for a heavy landing," the pilot said over the speakers, but no one listens. Instead they continue to watch Michael helping to land the plane.

"Okay, okay, okay!" Michael says as the plane quickly descends towards the ground. "Oh, this may hurt!"

The plane's wheels eject out preparing for landing, but Michael stays calm.

"Almost there, almost there!" he mutters as he can almost touch the ground.

BANG! SCREECH!

The plane strikes the tarmac and so does Michael as the ground impact dislodges him off the damaged wing. His body tears up a bit of the runway as he crashes and bounces away from the plane. Disorientated, Michael lies on the tarmac and watches the plane slow down with all wheels fully on the ground.

"Thank God!" he says exhaustedly, then he lies back and gazes up at the sky.

Everyone inside the plane cheers and hugs one another. Some cry and some finish their prayers. The children look out their windows, trying to catch another glimpse of Michael. The doors are opened and an inflatable slide is activated for the passengers as there is still risk of another explosion from the remaining engine.

Michael comes to his senses as he hears the sirens of the emergency vehicles in the distance.

"Well, that's my cue to leave," he groans and slowly rises back to his feet.

"Oh look, there he is!" some of the disembarked passengers say. They watch in awe as his wings spread out in their full glory, then as emergency vehicles approach the tarmac. he raises his wings upright and launches himself into the air. Everyone gasps and tries to record him on their mobile phones. The gust of wind from Michael's wings is so powerful they all stumble backwards a step or two.

"We have just missed the landing of Boeing 777, but as you can see the mystery hero has left the scene," the news reporter says from their vehicle which has just arrived on the tarmac. The cameraman does his best to zoom in on Michael, but he is just a speck on the screen.

"YES!" Father Brian yells and jumps about the presbytery.

"My Sweet Lord!" Cardinal Joseph breathes after witnessing the rescue live on his television. "Is this what you were referring to, Father Brian?"

"Yes, Your Eminence. And he is ready," he said smiling proudly.

"Who is he?"

"His name is Michael."

"This does changes everything!" Cardinal Joseph says as he blesses himself and sheds a tear. "I never lost faith, I never lost faith!" Father Brian hears the cardinal whisper through the phone while still mesmerised by the sight on TV. "This is great news, Father Brian. It will give everyone hope."

"There is one thing you should know, Cardinal Joseph."

"What is it?"

"Before this event, Michael wanted to keep his identity a secret. He was unsure of himself and worried about taking up the role and its enduring responsibilities."

"He has a duty to uphold!" the Cardinal responds in a stern voice. "He must take ownership of the gifts that have been given to him! You must make him realise this, Father Brian,"

"Yes, but—"

"No! You must do this."

"Michael has a family,!" Father Brian blurts.

For a moment there is silence, then the Cardinal said, "We all must make sacrifices during these uncertain times. I will check back on you later in the week. I trust you will not fail."

"I will do my best, Your Eminence," Father Brian replies, resigned.

"Good!" the Cardinal replies and hangs up the phone.

Kelly enters her home with bags of groceries in hand and sees Michael flying off into the distance on the television. "What the fudge!"

"Isn't it cool, Mum?" Emma says excitedly.

"What happened?"

"This guy here," she points to the speck on the screen, "everyone's saying he's an angel. The plane was going to crash, until he came and saved everyone."

"Wow" Kelly forces a lame response, her mind racing.

"That's all you have to say, Mum? This is *big*! It's like the world has a superhero now."

Chapter 15

Intel

Michael quietly opens the garage door leading into the kitchen. He has Kelly's flowers with him, but the cellophane wrapping is making more noise than him.

"DAD!" Both boys come racing to hug their father and wrap their arms around him tightly.

"Hey, boys!" he says as he hugs them back. "Where's mum?"

"She is in the bedroom," Hudson responds.

"Okay, I'm going to talk to mum. You boys okay being in the lounge?"

"Yep, Yep!" they both say as they skip off to the lounge.

"Hun?" Michael yells out.

"In here!" Kelly calls from their room, sounding irritable.

Michael cautiously approaches their room and sees Kelly sitting on their bed with her arms folded.

"Ah! You saw the news, didn't you?"

"Everyone saw the news!" she yells.

"I don't understand. Are you angry that I saved people?"

"No, I love that you saved those people," Kelly replies as she stands and takes the flowers from Michael. "Thanks for these, by the way. I am proud of you, but you got caught on camera! Look!"

She shows him the social media feed on her phone. He takes Kelly's phone and views the footage himself. Every post shows Michael flying off or standing up with his wings spread out. "Yeah, but, all these images of me are unclear and from a distance."

"It only takes one computer geek to take the unclear footage and spit out a clean image," Kelly points out. "By the end of the week the whole world will know who you are!!"

"I'll wear a mask next time," he promises his wife, hoping to calm her down. Kelly turns her back on him and places one hand on her hip and the other against her forehead while she sighs.

"Kel, I'm sorry, it's just—"

"It's happening so quickly," Kelly continues. "I always knew it was bound to happen, but I just didn't realise it would be so soon. You are about to be the most famous person in the entire world. Are you ready for that? 'Cos I'm not and neither is this family."

Michael knew she was right. His once peaceful life was about to be dragged into the spotlight. There was so much evil in the world that he would barely be able to spend time with his family or have a sit-down family meal ever again. This realisation hits Michael hard.

The doorbell rings and he jumps in alarm. "What! Who is that?"

"Dinner," Kelly replies wearily. "I ordered pizza. I'm not cooking dinner tonight; I feel too tired."

"Okay, I'll get the delivery and grab some plates," Michael offers, then as he heads for the front door he shouts, "KIDS! PIZZA!"

"Oh, yes, PIZZA!" Hudson shouts out loud, running into the dining room. Isaiah follows behind mimicking his older brother, "Oh, yes, PIZZA!"

Emma is already sitting at the dinner table. "Yay, Pizza!" she says as she waves her hands in the air, mocking her brothers.

"Ok, everybody sit," Kelly commands as Michael brings in the pizzas. She hands a Cheese Lover pizza to the kids. "There you go."

Michael takes a slice of his and Kelly's Meat Lovers and says "So how was everyones day?" He's trying to keep some normalcy; he and Kelly grin at one another.

"All of my friends are talking about that new hero!" Emma gushes.

"A hero?" Isaiah replies.

"What? Where Emma?" Hudson asks.

"On the news. He saved a plane from crashing!"

"Whoa! Cool" the boys reply in unison, then Hudson realises, "So, wait, that means he can fly?"

"Yes."

"Wow! What you think of him?"

"Or her," Michael suggests as he looks over at his wife who shakes her head.

"He was cool and had huge wings," Emma continued, "but no one could get a good look at him and the news reporters were late on the scene. Actually, he looked a little like you, Dad."

"That's pretty cool, hey guys?" Michael adds with a grin.

"Stop!" Kelly says abruptly to Michael. "I don't want you to encourage them."

"Sorry, Hun" Michael apologises, but Emma comes to the aid of her father. "Mum, this guy is big news! I think the world is going to change now that he has come to help us."

Kelly gives Michael a look as if to say, 'I told you so.'

"Yeah, but what if this guy has other priorities?"

"Huh, what do you mean, Dad?"

"Well, what if he has a family? We shouldn't put all our faith in him."

"If he is a hero and he does have a family, then I'm sure his family would understand and let him save people and the world," Emma replies.

Kelly looks at Michael and gives him an exhausted, broken smile. The family continued to eat their pizza in silence unaware that the hero they were talking about was sitting at the dinner table with them.

Later that night, a bus parks underneath the bridge of the busy freeway and a horde of newly formed soldiers climb down from it. Constable Sacks is the last to leave the bus. As she exits, she draws a big sigh and reaches for her mobile phone.

"Master, I have something to show you!"

"What is it?"

"Here." Megan shows the creature the footage of Michael saving the plane earlier today.

"So, he has FINALLY showed himself!"

"Is this good news?" Megan asks.

"Not good news, but intel," the creature replies. "We knew we wouldn't go undetected entering into this realm. We also knew that there would be repercussions. Therefore, we have been entrusted to build this army you now see before you."

"What intel can we gather from this footage?" Megan asks.

"Not much as the footage is bad, but those are no ordinary wings. They are bigger than your average angel wings which means we have attracted the attention of an archangel. The question is, which one?"

"Does it matter which one?"

"YES, OF COURSE IT MATTERS!" the creatures shouts at Megan. "There is only one Angel I fear and that angel is the only one that rivals our Boss!"

Megan is shocked to discover that her master has a fear and that there is an angel out there with such power that he could turn the tide for the humans.

Chapter 16

The Cavalry

A new day has dawned. Michael slowly gets out of bed, trying hard not to wake his wife. He opens his bedside drawer and finds his arthritis medication for his knees. However, as he bends down for it, he notices there is no pain or awkwardness in his knees.

"Hmm!" he mutters to himself. He places the medication back in the drawer and closes it, then he makes his way to the kitchen and starts to make everyone's breakfast. Michael cooks up a batch of pancakes then makes coffee for Kelly and himself.

Both boys race out of their bedroom at precisely six o'clock.

"Good morning, Dad! Thanks, Dad!" they both shout, then they take their breakfast into the lounge, racing to see who sits down first.

"I win!" Isaiah shouts as he jumps onto the lounge chair.

"No! I win!" Hudson retorts.

"No! Hudson, you need to have your tablet with you as well!"

"Isaiah, you can't just make up a rule!" Hudson protests.

"Okay, boofheads, just eat your breakfast!" Michael scolds them, shaking his head

"Hey Dad, did you know it's Christmas Eve?" Hudson asks.

"Yes, I know."

"Oh, okay. Just saying because there are no presents from you and Mum under the Christmas tree."

"Yes, your mother and I will sort that out later today, okay?"

"Okay."

"Ah!" Michael sighs as he sits on his own chair in the sitting room that is sectioned off from the dining room. He places his coffee down on the coffee table, reaches for the remote and turns on the TV to watch the morning news. He lowers the volume so he doesn't wake his wife.

The news reporter announces, *'Dash-cam footage has captured the moment a speeding car lost control and recklessly endangered the oncoming traffic in the opposite lane during the night.'*

Michael gasps and whispers to himself, "What in the name…?"

He races to the bedroom to wake his wife. "Kel?" He shakes her gently. "Kel! Kel!"

"WHAT?" she shouts angrily.

"Quick, come with me!"

"No!"

"Please, please, come with me" he pleads. "You have to see this!"

"Oh, this had better be good," she warns him as she reluctantly gets out of bed.

He guides her to the sitting room and points to the TV. "Look!"

Kelly sits down in her lounge chair beside Michael.

"This footage has not been edited and as you can see both cars had dash cams," the news reporter told his world-wide viewers. A female angel steps between both cars and uses her wings to cushion them for a minimal impact.

"After two angel sightings this poses the question—are there more out there?" the reporter concludes

"Good question," Michael says out loud while Kelly is speechless. Eventually she whispers to her husband, "There are more of you?"

"It looks like it."

"WOW!" Kelly says as she watches the footage of the female angel. "Who is she, I wonder?"

"I don't know, but I think I should find out" Michael replies. "This whole thing started when I was struck by lightning. What if she was too? That lightning show lasted for nearly two minutes, so more people could have been struck. However—" Michael ponders

"What is it?" Kelly prompts.

"Father Brian did say I was one of the lucky ones who survived. Does that mean some were struck by lightning and didn't make it?"

"I don't know, but you need to find out somehow, Michael."

"How?"

"Look it up," Kelly suggested. "It was a big event so it might say online how many casualties there were that night."

"Good idea!" Michael rushes over to their computer desk with his coffee. "Okay, lightning storm incident," he says out loud as he types.

Michael reads one of the headlines: 'The natural disaster that stopped a country'

Curious, he clicks on the link and reads through the report whispering every word under his breath, then he tells Kelly, "No other country seemed to be affected by the event. It was as if we were targeted. The total death toll is unclear, but one hundred and ten people are recorded as dying from their wounds after being struck. Good God!" he exclaims. "There's nothing about any survivors."

"Well, go to the next report then," Kelly tells him.

"Ah, this one looks promising: 'What really happened on the night of the 7th of December'. It was a lightning show like no other," he mutters under his breath as he reads the article. "Over a hundred people died due to this phenomenon, but according to hospital records seven people survived this ordeal. Kel!" he shouts. "There are seven survivors!"

"Wow! Really?" Kelly says as she approaches him at the computer desk. "I don't suppose it has their names?"

"No, it doesn't."

"Hold on!" Kelly says, tapping Michael on his shoulder, "How many important angels are there?"

"You mean the Archangels?"

"Well, yeah. I wonder, do you think there would be seven?"

"Um, I don't…" Michael begins, then he asks, "Where's my Bible?"

"Just look it up on the computer."

Michael types into the search engine: 'How many Archangels are there?'

"Wow!" Kelly exclaims as she sits beside Michael to read the results of his search.

"They have their names and what they do or responsible for. Gabriel is the messenger of God; Raphael is the healer and guide; Uriel is the light of God; Selaphiel is connected to prayers or worship; Raguel is the friend of God who oversees justice and fairness; Barachiel is the guardian of the faithful and finally, Michael. He is the leader of Heaven's army and the protector of Humanity." Kelly looks at her husband admiringly and says, "You have a BIG RESPONSIBILITY, babe!"

"Yeah, you think?!" Michael jokes.

"So, seven survivors. What's the bet that these seven survivors have inherited the traits of the seven Archangels?"

"Something's coming!" Michael whispers aloud

"Did you say something?" Kelly asks.

"I think something bad is coming."

"I think that something is already here, babe," Kelly replies. "Or did you forget about the Pope and that strange horse cloud?"

"Yeah, but when I spoke with God—"

"I'm sorry, what?" Kelly interjected.

"I must have forgotten to tell you."

"Uh, yeah, you did!" she scolds him.

"The other night when I said I was speaking to the neighbour, I was actually talking to Him!"

"I see," Kelly responds in an annoyed manner.

"I'm sorry," Michael apologises. "I didn't know how to tell you it was Him."

"Ok, anyway, what did He say?"

"He explained why He chose me and told me that I was chosen BECAUSE something is coming."

"And…?"

"That's it. You turned on the outside lights asking if someone was there. I called out to you and when I turned back, He was gone!"

"Argh!" Kelly says in frustration. "That's not much to go on!"

"Well, it confirms that something is coming."

"Really?" Kelly says sarcastically. "You couldn't figure that out from the message left by the Pope's killers?"

"What's wrong?" Michael asks.

"Aren't you a little annoyed at not knowing what is currently happening?" Kelly shouts. "It annoys me that we don't know a thing! I feel something bad is about to happen and we won't know what until it actually happens! What if it was something you could have prevented?"

"Hun, I can only do what I can see in front of me," Michael explains. "If God wanted me to do more, He should have told me instead of being cryptic about it."

"Yes, but that's being reactive to a situation," Kelly protests. "If someone gets badly hurt or something else tragically happens and you could have done something about it, can you live with that?"

Michael lowers his head and thinks for a moment, then as he walks to their bedroom; Kelly follows behind.

"Babe, you okay?" she asks as he stares out the window.

He turns around to face his wife and replies, "I still think they've chosen the wrong person for the job. My whole heart is not fully into this new gig. I feel that it's a part-time job, especially now that we know there are more angels out there."

"Yeah, but—" Kelly begins, but Michael interrupts her.

"No, 'buts'. You and the kids are my main priority," he says as he approaches her and places both his hands on her hips. He then gives her a kiss for reassurance.

"I'm regretting buying you an outfit," Kelly whispers.

"What? You got me an *outfit*?"

"Yeah, but Mum is making some alterations to it."

"I'll still wear it for you, hun," Michael promises as he hugs her again for the thoughtful gesture.

Chapter 17

The Possession

The police station was inundated. Every phone was busy and every chair occupied by people waiting to be seen by a police officer as if it were the emergency ward of a hospital. Some are rude and yell at those on the front counter, some are crying, not knowing what to do next or where to go from here.

"Everyone please bear with us," a constable returning to the front desk calls out, "as you can see we have a lot of people to get through today!"

"Sergeant, we have another missing person," another constable tells Sergeant Andrew Mourning, who is standing in front of a whiteboard with the photos of hundreds of missing people on it.

"What in God's name is going on?" he mutters as he scratches his chin. "Something strange is happening here, I just can't see it!" He turns around and sees his station in chaos as every officer tries to attend to the distressed and disorderly members of the public.

"Sergeant, Sergeant! We have the news on line four wanting a statement."

"No!"he says firmly. "No, press. Not yet. We need to figure out what's going on here first."

"Right, sir!"

"This is too much!" Sergeant Mourning whispers to himself as he rests a hand on his head for comfort. "It's only ten in the morning and we still have the rest of the day to get through." He takes a deep breath and locks himself away in his office.

***

On the other side of town, Father Brian blesses himself and kneels in front of a statue of the Virgin Mary in the church. Bowing his head he whispers, "Michael, please hear my prayer."

Michael is helping Kelly wrap presents and place them under the Christmas tree when he suddenly hears a loud voice in his head. Closing his eyes tightly he listens to the voice.

"Michael, please hear my prayer," Father Brian's voice tells him. *"I need to talk with you now. Please come see me at the church."*

"WHAT WAS THAT?" Michael cries out loud.

"What was what?" Kelly replies, baffled.

"Um, I think I heard a prayer."

"Really?" Kelly exclaims. "That's cool!"

"It was Father Brian. He wants to speak with me at the church."

"It might be important," Kelly replies as she places the presents under the Christmas tree, "I'm good here, you should go and see what he wants."

"You're sure?" Michael asks.

"Yeah, I'm good."

Michael drives to the church. As it's Christmas Eve there are barely any cars on the road so he's able to get to the church quickly.

"I hope I wasn't hearing things," Michael says to himself, noting there are no cars in the church carpark. He exits his vehicle and makes his way to the deserted church to find that the doors are already open.

He enters the church and calls out for Father Brian.

"Ah, Michael!" Father Brian says as he pops his head from out from the sacristy door. "Come, come!"

He ushers him into the room and gestures for him to sit down before a table with a folder on it.

"So, it was you that was talking to me through a prayer?" Michael asks.

"You heard it?" Father Brian exclaims. "I wasn't sure if it was going to work."

"Yeah, it did, but it was weird."

"Sorry, I wouldn't have done so if it wasn't important."

"Why? What's going on, Father?"

"Well," Father Brian says as he opens the folder on the table. "This is Maddie, short for Madeline." He takes out a photo and shows Michael a picture of a twelve-year-old girl

"Her mother, Maria, is one of my many loyal parishioners. She rang me last night. Her daughter was a very sprightful girl who had a lot of life—"

"Had? Was?" Michael notes. "Those are past tense. Is Maddie okay?"

"Well, that's it—we don't know," Father Brian replies.

"What do you mean?"

"There's no easy way to tell you this, so I'm just going to say it" Father Brian says firmly. "Maria believes her daughter has been possessed by a demon."

"What!" Michael cries as he rises to his feet. "Do you believe her?"

"I'm a priest. I have to listen. Besides, I was going to make my way to their house today and check for myself, but…I was hoping to take you with me to see them."

"Do you think that's a good idea, Father?" Michael asks.

"Yes, I do," Father Brian replies, "If it is true that she's possessed, having you there would put me at ease."

Michael thinks about it, then he sighs, "Okay."

"Great!" Father Brian replies happily. "Let's go! My car is parked out the back."

Michael follows the priest to his car and is surprised by his choice of vehicle. "I didn't peg you for the sporty SUV vehicle type, Father," Michael jokes.

"There's a lot you don't know about me."

"Oh, really?"

"Yep, for starters," he says as turns on his car, "The only music that gets played in my car is COUNTRY!"

"My kind of music," Michael says with a smile.

The pair bob their heads along to the country music on the car radio. Twenty minutes later Michael begins to get restless. "I don't want to sound like my son, but are we there yet, Father?"

Father Brian laughs. "Very nearly," he says with a smile. "I think this is their street. We are looking for number six."

"Is that it there?" Michael asks pointing towards a house on the left side of the street. "It looks like a normal house."

"What were you expecting, fire and brimstone?" Father Brian says as he pulls into the driveway. "Now, I will do all the talking," Father Brian says as he knocks on the door.

"I wasn't going to say much anyway" Michael replies, then Maria opens the door.

"Hello Maria," Father Brian says gently.

"I wasn't expecting you to bring company, Father," Maria replies as she eyes Michael warily.

"Yes, sorry for not discussing that with you. This is my helper, Michael."

"Nice to meet you, Maria," Michael says as he shakes her hand

"Nice to meet you as well. I'm sure Father has informed you of my situation. I'm a little on edge right now."

"That's okay, I understand" Michael soothes her. "We will try our best to help."

"Thank you," she replies as she lets them both into her house and shuts the door.

"Where is Maddie now?" Father Brian asks.

"She is in her room," Maria says as she points down the corridor of her house. "It's the last one on the right."

"Okay," Father Brian replies, then he gives Michael a hand signal to follow him.

"I smell something, Father," Michael whispers.

"Do you know what it is?"

"No, not really. It's like something rotten, almost like—"

"EGGS!" they both exclaim at the same time.

"That's sulphur," Father Brian tells Michael.

"Really? So, you smell it too?"

"No, I can't smell it, but I have been told that sulphur has an odour similar to rotten eggs."

"So, does that mean…"

"Yes, we are dealing with a DEMON!" Father answers Michael's unfinished question. "Be on guard and ready for anything."

They give each other a nod before Father Brian opens the door. Madeline is lying on her bed with her eyes closed listening to music through her headphones.

"She looks so normal," Michael notes.

"Don't let it fool you," Father Brian whispers, then he gently taps Madeline's foot. She opens her eyes and sees Father Brian and a stranger peering down at her.

"Father Brian!" she exclaims as she sits up on her bed, then keeping a watchful eye on Michael she asks sternly, "Who is he?"

"This is my helper, Michael."

"It's nice to meet you," Michael says as he extends his hand, but she shrinks away from him and curls herself up on the corner of her bed.

"What's the matter, Maddie?" Father Brian asks curiously.

"I don't like him!"

"Why?"

"Mummy!" Madeline yells out. "Where are you, Mum?"

Michael awkwardly backs away.

"Mummy's here, baby!" Maria cries as she rushes to her aid

"Stop!" Father Brian says abruptly, raising his hand. Maria stays at the door.

"Maddie, can you tell me why you don't like my friend here?" the priest asks, pointing towards Michael.

"This is a trap!" Maddie declares, her voice suddenly assuming a deep demonic quality.

Michael is spooked by the change in her voice and Madeline's mother begins to cry as this confirms her fears that her child is possessed.

"Maddie, look at me" Father Brian says in a firm voice, "I'm going to get my friend here to place his hand on your forehead, okay?"

"NO!" Maddie yells out loud.

"Please Maddie. Just for a second, I promise." Father Brian nods to Michael to give him the go ahead. Michael nods back and slowly approaches Maddy who is curled up against the wall on her bed.

"No, stay away!" Maddie yells at Michael. "Mummy, why aren't you doing anything?"

"Baby, I'm right here," Maria cries.

"Maddie, please calm down," Father Brian says calmly.

"No! No! STOP!" Madeline screams as Michael holds one of her flailing arms. His other hand is just about to touch her forehead when Maddie's eyes begin to glow bright yellow. Her chest is upright and her head droops back. Michael catches her head as she passes out.

"Good catch," Father Brian whispers to Michael.

"Thanks," he replies, then Maria tells Michael, "I know what you are!"

Michael and Father Brian turned around and see Maria also has glowing yellow eyes.

"WHAT?" Michael exclaims in shock.

"Easy, Michael" Father Brian said. "It's moved on to the next host."

"MICHAEL!" Maria said in a demonic voice. "Master will be pleased to hear what I have to say."

"Michael, she must not escape," Father Brian whispers.

"Right," Michael replies as he gently lowers Madeline's head back down on her bed, then he turned to face the demon within Maria. "Listen, I don't know who you are or what you want—"

"We want Eden back!" the demon cried.

"Eden?" Michael replied, confused.

"YES! We inherited Eden at the dawn of time."

"Demons once lived on Earth?" Michael asks.

"No! We were all angels once. Demons only came into existence when He defied God!"

"You're talking about Lucifer?" Father Brian interrupts.

"Yes! Who else, *FATHER*?" the demon replies in a snide manner. "When He defied God, we rallied behind him. Unfortunately, when God damned Lucifer his followers were also damned. Our new home is what you humans call HELL! He turned us all into demons. Imagine a place that amplifies your sins. Here on Eden, we can feed off your sins like they are chocolate with no repercussions, but in Hell they feed on you until there isn't an ounce of your angel essence left. You are left disfigured and unrecognisable!"

"I guess it pays to not go against God!" Michael quips.

"THIS WAS OUR HOME!" the demon shouted, "AND WE WANT IT BACK!"

"Well, you can't," Michael says defiantly as he steps towards the demon.

"Who's going to stop us? You?"

"Yes, me," Michael replied as he takes another step towards the demon

"Not another step!" The demon makes Maria reach for her head, with one hand under her chin and the other behind her head. "I will snap her neck right here and now!"

"Okay, okay!" Michael quickly takes two steps backwards and is now side by side with Father Brian.

"Lower her hands," Michael commands the demon.

"Argh!" the demon groans as it lowers Maria's hands to her sides.

"Okay, what do you want?" Michael asks.

The demon is silent. It stands there hauntingly staring at Father Brian and Michael.

"What would it take for you to leave this vessel?" the priest asked.

"You're obviously not a real Angel," the demon tells Michael.

"Why would you say that?" he replies.

Because a TRUE angel knows their worth!" It takes a step into the bedroom with confidence, "And you are unsure of yourself!"

"You don't know me," Michael interrupts

"I know you better than your own wife…Kelly, isn't it?"

"Shut up!" Michael shouts.

"Father, did you know that this so-called angel doesn't even want the gifts that were bestowed upon him?"

"What?" Father Brian murmurs, looking at Michael

"Yes, his inherited gifts are going to waste," the demon continues. "If it was up to him, this FAKE angel would give up his gifts in a split second, leaving humanity defenceless!"

"I SAID SHUT—!" Michael yells as he takes a step towards the demon, who once again raises Marias hands getting ready to snap her neck.

"Okay!" Michael says as he raises his own hands and slowly takes a step backwards.

"What do you want?" Father Brian said firmly.

"I WANT TO KNOW THE NAME OF THE ANGEL THAT GAVE THEIR ESSENCE TO YOU!" the demon shouted at Michael. "It will please my Master."

"It was no angel; it was God!"

"Ha-ha-ha-ha! You don't know, do you?"

"WHAT?" Michael asked as he tried to creep forward.

"This is just delightful!" The demon growls a laugh, so pleased with itself. Just then Michael lunged for Maria and grabbed hold of her hands.

"Gotcha!"

"Argh!" the demon shrieked as Maria's eyes glowed bright yellow, then it left Maria's body which collapsed. Fortunately, Michael caught her before she landed on the floor.

"Another good catch," Father Brian says.

"Thanks," Michael replies, then Madeline finally begins to stir.

"Mummy? What happened, Father?" Her small voice is terrified as she spots her mother.

"She's okay, Maddie," Father Brian comforts her.

Michael lifts Maria and carries her into the lounge where he lays her down on the three-seater sofa.

"That was a lot to digest," Michael says to Father Brian as he rises back to his feet.

"Hmm!"

"What's wrong, Father?"

"What's this stuff about you giving up your gifts?"

"Come on, you're going to listen to a demon?"

"Well, was it lying?"

"Um…"

"That's what I thought!" Father Brian replies with disappointment in his voice as he sits down on a one-seater sofa. "I don't understand why you would want to give up a gift like this?"

"This gift is fine!" Michael says as he sits down across from Father Brian and tries to find a way to explain his feelings. "It's just the job itself and the responsibilities that come with it. It expects you to put your life on the line for the sake of others.”

“And you don’t want to do that?”

“It’s not that I am afraid of dying,” Michael replied, “but I have kids, and I wish to see them grow up and live their own lives. Maybe see what my grandchildren would look like.” As his eyes begin to well up he adds, “I love seeing my kids grow up; it’s the highlight of my life. It’s what keeps me going,” he finishes as he wipes his tears away from his face.

“Oh, my boy!” Father Brian says with sadness in his voice. “A hero’s life is difficult, one filled with sacrifices, but think of all the other fathers you will save and mothers that want to see their own kids grow up. They need you so they can go back to their families as well.”

Michael concedes that Father Brian has an interesting point. He wipes away his tears and says, “You have a way with words, Father.”

“It’s my specialty,” Father Brian jokes and the two share a laugh.

Maria slowly comes to and asks, “What’s going on?”

“Mummy!” Madeline rushes over to her mother and gives her a hug

“Where am I, Father? What happened?”

“You’re still in your home and Maddie is safe!” Father Brian replies.

“My head’s a little fuzzy. I remember opening the door for you, Father, but it gets jumbled from there. Can I get some water?”

“I’ll get it,” Michael offers and heads off to the kitchen.

Father Brian helps Maria to sit upright and tells her quietly, "We managed to chase the demon out of Maddie."

"Oh good!" Maria says with relief.

"However, it latched itself onto you."

"What!" Maria cries, horrified. "Is it gone now?"

"We think so," Father Brian assures her then Michael returns and hands a glass of water to Maria saying, "Here you go."

"Thank you," Maria replies, then she downs the glass of water within seconds.

"Thirsty?" Father Brian asks.

"For some reason, yes," Maria acknowledges.

"Michael, can you feel her forehead for a temperature?" Father Brian asks.

"Uh, okay." Michael obliges and places a hand over her forehead. "All good," he declares as he steps away, giving Maria some space.

"Seems so," Father Brian whispers under his breath.

"Huh?"

"Oh nothing, I was just testing Maria to see if the demon was actually gone," Father Brian explains, "because for some reason the demon was not too keen on your touch, Michael."

"That's right!" Maria says as her memory begins to come back to her. "I remember being possessed; it was like I was a passenger in my own body. And for some reason it was VERY scared of you, even when it was trying to be confident."

Father Brian stands up and then proceeds to kneel in front of her. "Maria, can you recall anything else that maybe of some use to us?"

"Like what?" Maria asks.

"Where it lived? Are there others?"

Maria closes her eyes and concentrates. "Oh, there is something; something which scared me to my core! When that thing said its MASTER, it recalled a memory of its Master! I could not fully see where or what it was, but the vision I saw was of a dark and gloomy place. There were these creatures all around moaning and groaning, then suddenly a huge silhouette of a creature stood upright and looked right at me with dark red eyes."

Maria begins to tremble.

"It's okay," Michael says, trying to comfort her. "It was just a vision."

"No, I don't think it was."

"Why do you say that, Maria?" Michael asks.

"Because the creature was under a bridge. I think they're here!" she sobs and trembles uncontrollably

"Hey, it's okay," Father Brian said as he places a reassuring hand over her own.

"That's not what's troubling me the most, Father."

Father Brian and Michael look at each other, worried what her next words were going to be.

"That demon did not fear God at all! And not because of arrogance, but because it's convinced there is no God."

"Everything is going to be okay, Maria," Father Brian smiles at her.

"Father, how is everything going to be okay?"

"I take it you have missed the news this past week. Who could blame you? Your daughter had your full attention. But you see him," he points towards Michael, "he is going to show you why that demon was so afraid of him and why God does exist."

"But what about my identity?" Michael whispers to Father Brian.

"She needs this, Michael!" Father Brian whispers back, patting him on the shoulder.

Michael nods his head at Father Brian and prepares himself by standing with his feet apart. Maddie jumps onto her mother's lap as they both watch Michael. He makes a slight dip in his shoulders and as he does his wings eject outwards. They rip away his shirt and spread out, but not to their full length, for Michael is cautious of the confined space of the house.

"WOW!" Maddie yells out loud.

"OH, MY GOODNESS!" Maria gasps as she covers her mouth with both hands, shocked by what she is witnessing. Maddy laughs and begins to play with the feathers.

"There is a God!" Maria says cheerfully and in an instant all her fears melt away. She had found happiness when there was none and all because she knew what Michael was. He smiles at the mother and daughter, bonding as they brush his wings, then he looks over at Father Brian and they both share a smile. Michael nods to him as he finally accepts his role was to be Eden's champion.

Michael and Father Brian arrive back to the church. As they get out of the priest's car, Michael says gratefully, "Thanks for today, Father."

"No, thank you, Michael. I couldn't have done it without you!" Father Brian replies. "That family deserved to be saved, especially after the year they had. Maria's ex-husband took everything from her."

"I'm glad we've done this," Michael said, "it was a blessing in disguise! It was what I needed, and I enjoyed seeing their faces when they saw my wings." He smiles as he recollects this moment. "That's a memory I will cherish!"

"I'm glad," Father Brian replies, "because we need you more than ever." He turns to face his church and leans his back against his car. "There was one thing that Maria said which disturbed me."

"What is it, Father?"

"Maria said she thinks they are already here. What if Hell's Army is already here on Earth?"

"Come on!" Michael replies with a snort. "Don't you think we would have seen or noticed something? Or at the very least seen destruction here and there?"

"You did save a plane from the skies," Father Brian reminds him. "If not for you, that would have been disastrous. A lot of families would have been in mourning right now."

Michael is lost for words.

"Look Michael, all I'm saying is don't let your guard down," Father Brian suggests. "Maybe you should do a patrol here and there, keep an eye out."

"I'll consider it," Michael replies as he walks over to his own car.

"Please do!" Father Brian yells out to Michael as he hops into his car and gives him a cheeky salute. "I mean it!"

Chapter 18

Casualties

In a darkened tunnel Constable Sacks treads towards a horde of beastly beings fighting amongst each other, growling and snarling.

"We are almost ready!" the creature tells Megan

"Is there anything you need me to do in the meantime, Master?"

"Yes, I need you to draw out this Angel," the creature says, "we need to know more about him."

"I can do that," she replies. Just then a homeless man runs out from one of the sewage tunnels crying and shrieking for the Master.

"WHO IS IT?" the creature shouts.

"It is I, Gazlien," the homeless man replies as he kneels before the creature.

"What do you want?"

"I bring you news on the angel," Gazlien says as he stands upright. "I possessed a child in a suburb far north from here."

"AND?" the creature yells impatiently.

"One of the Almighty's foot soldiers came to disarm me and brought an angel with him."

"An angel?" the creature interrupts.

"Yes, an angel," Gazlien confirms.

"WHAT WAS HIS NAME?"

"I do not know his actual Angel name…" Gazlien replies, not meeting his Master's eyes "…but the foot soldier that was with him called him by his human name,"Gazlien added.

"What was it?" the creature asks, his back turned.

"MICHAEL!" Gazlien snarls.

"Michael…!" the creature repeats, then he muses to himself, "I wonder... SLAVE!"

"Yes, Master?" Megan is instantly at his side.

"Head north and find out all you can about this *Michael*"

"But how? I don't know what he looks like?"

"DRAW HIM OUT!" the creature shouts. "We can't advance until we know what we are dealing with!"

"Right!" Megan obediently sets off to do his bidding.

"GAZLIEN!"

"Yes, Master?"

"You have proven yourself. Come with me."

"Of course, Master!" Gazlien replies, then he follows him deep inside the sewers until finally they arrive at an open section. Ahead of them were three tunnels with sunlight streaming in from the sewerage grate above.

"You are going to prove yourself further, Gazlien," the creature says. "I am too big to travel any further, but I want you to do something for me."

"Anything, Master," Gazlien agrees, loyal to the cause.

The creature explains his sinister plan in detail to Gazlien, who laughs murderously.

"You understand the plan?"

"Yes, Master," Gazlien agrees

"At the end of this tunnel you will find an exit. NOW GO!"

Gazlien dashes away and disappears into the dark tunnel ahead. The creature snarls as it sits down in the sewerage waiting for daylight to pass and for Gazlien to complete his mission.

***

The day comes to an end and the once busy police station is nearly empty. "Thank God today is over!" Sergeant Mourning says to himself as he packs up his desk and grabs his coat off the rack in his office.

"Sarge!" an officer yells out after hanging up the phone. "There's a disturbance in the city square!"

"What's going on?"

"A homeless man is running rampant, sir."

"That's a patrolman's duty," the sergeant says in annoyance.

"You don't understand Sarge. He's killed three people."

"WHAT!" Sergeant Mourning exclaims. "How many of our officers are on the scene?"

"We have two patrol cars enroute as we speak!"

"Good! I'll head out there now," Sergeant Mourning calls as he throws on his jacket.

"Yes, sir!"

"No rest for the wicked," the Sergeant sighs to himself as he heads out of the station.

Screams are heard throughout the city square as panicked people race for cover in the nearby nightclubs and shops. Dead bodies lie on the street and the assailant is still on the loose.

An evil laugh, almost comical in its pitch, yet still eerie, echoes through a nearby alley way. Everyone screams and runs aimlessly again, then the flap of wings is heard from above.

"Here they come!" Gazlien murmurs to himself. He then shows himself and tries to find another human victim.

"Look! They've come to save us!" a bystander shouts as they point up into the air.

"There's two of them!" another observes.

"The more the merrier," Gazlien jokes to himself, then he grabs hold of one of the bystanders pointing to the sky.

"HELP!" she shouts, "Please don't hurt me!"

Gazlien looks up at the sky and tries to get a glimpse of the angels.

"Where are you?" he whispers, then a voice commands, "Let her go!"

Gazlien is spooked, for the voice is coming from behind him in the darkened alleyway.

"Sure!" Gazlien said as he places two hands over the young lady's head. "First, how about you and your friend show yourself?"

Gazlien and the lady watch the alleyway carefully, then some movement can be seen in the darkness. A colour of murky grey slowly emerges as an angel comes into the light.

His wings are white and as he stands before them he demands, "LET HER GO!"

"Not until your friend comes out!" Gazlien retorted. "I know there are two of you!"

"Here I am!" Another angel lands behind Gazlien, only this one is female.

"What a lovely couple!" he taunts them.

"You don't know us!" the male angel shouts.

"I know your name is Adam!" Gazlien said as he grins menacingly at him.

"WHAT?" Adam exclaims, surprised.

"And your girlfriend over there is Abigail! But I wonder which angel you are both descend from?"

"What do you mean?" Abigail asks.

"Which angel's essence do you have in your blood?" Gazlien explains

"Adam, could this mean we were chosen?" Abigail asks

Adam's reply is sharp. "Not now."

Gazlien smirks, thinking to himself how foolish they are to believe they will live beyond the next 5 minutes. He turns and calls for his Master, who he knows must be waiting nearby.

"Looks likes you were set up!" Adam said as he steps towards Gazlien, who is feverishly looking around for his Master, who has failed to appear.

"Get back!" he says as he digs his rotten fingernails deep into the lady's skin drawing some blood from her neck. "Master!" He calls.

Adam stops, seeing the blood, and says, "Take it easy!"

"MASTER!" Gazlien continues to yell while Abigail slowly approaches Gazlien from behind. She looks over at her boyfriend and nods.

"Listen, why don't you let her go and we can just talk?" Adam tries to reason with Gazlien, but he ignores him and continues to yell out loud, "MASTER!"

Police sirens can be heard quickly approaching their location.

"You hear that? It's over," Adam tells Gazlien who snarls and sneers at him.

"It's not over!"

"Yes, it is," Abigail says as she latches onto Gazlien's arm, freeing his hostage.

"RUN!" Abigail shouts to the lady.

"ARGHHHHH!" Gazlien yells as his eyes begin to glow yellow.

"Hey, calm down!" Abigail says as she grips him tighter.

"ARGH! AHHHH!" Gazlien continues to scream, then he passes out and his body droops.

"What happened?" Adam asks Abigail.

"I don't know," she replies as she lays Gazlien down on the pavement.

"You vaporised the demon within!" a monstrous voice replies out of nowhere. "An angel can kill a demon with only a touch!"

Both angels look around, trying to pinpoint where this voice is coming from.

"Adam, I'm scared!" Abigail whispers.

"It's okay, I'm here," he tried to reassure her as they both stand back-to-back. "There's nothing to be afraid of."

"You should be scared!" the voice taunts.

The sirens could now be heard more clearly as they were only a block away. The heavens rumble as rain begins to fall; odd, for the summer.

Both angels try to remain calm.

"Anything?" Adam asks Abigail.

"Nothing my end," she replies, then suddenly Adam is pulled away by one of his wings into one of the dark alleyways.

"ADAM!" Abigail cries out in alarm. "ADAM!"

From inside the alley Adam cries out in pain.

Abigail begins to weep as she watches the darkened alley for movement. The rain begins to pour down, as if the heavens are also weeping for Adam. His body is thrown out in front of Abigail. She kneels down and holds his head up. She can see his chest had been pierced by something. Placing a hand over the wound she cries uncontrollably and rests her head on his chest.

"So, angels aren't as indestructible as we thought!" the voice from the alley mocks.

"AARRGGHH!" Abigail screams at the voice, then she lays Adam's head back down and rises to her feet, ready for battle.

"Ah, still some fight left! the evil voice taunts. "GOOD!"

"AARRGGHH!" Abigail screams louder this time then she charges into the darkness, not waiting for the creature to show itself.

"IS ANYONE ON THE SCENE?" Sergeant Andrew Mourning yells into his dispatch radio.

"This is Constable Alonzo, sir. I have just arrived on scene and it's not pretty!"

"What street?"

"James Street."

"I'll be there soon!" the sergeant tells him before he places his radio back on the holder.

Sergeant Mourning arrives to find Constable Alonzo sitting on the pavement, his back turned towards the crime scene. Upon seeing the sergeant, he rises and begins to wipe some of his tears away.

"Sir!" Constable Alonzo croaks.

"My God! What happened here?" Sergeant Mourning gasps, for the crime scene is too much even for him. He drops to his knees, his feet unable to take the weight. News reporters arriving on the scene are also stunned. One of the camera operators makes the sign of the cross while a small figure watches the scene unfold but stays hidden near one of the corner buildings.

Chapter 19

The Aftermath

"MICHAEL, PLEASE HEAR MY PRAYER!" Father Brian prays desperately.

Michael squints his eyes shut at the table where he is eating dinner with his family, a low moan escapes his lips.

"What is it?" Kelly asks.

"Father Brian," Michael whispers to his wife, then he gets up from the dinner table and walks into the lounge.

"What?" Michael mutters to the priest.

"Whoa! I can hear you!" Father Brian replies, amazed.

"What do you want, Father?"

"Turn your TV on! QUICK!"

"Okay, Okay," Michael replies. He finds the remote control and turns on the TV; nothing could have prepared him for what he sees next. The news reporter is so focused on the slaying of two angels that he has totally forgotten about the human victims. The camera shows the two angels with their wings stretched out and pegged against a building in a crucifix position.

Michael begins to breathe heavily as his anger boils to the surface.

"Michael!" Father Brian calls, but he can only hear his own ragged breathing.

"MICHAEL!" the priest repeats only this time with urgency. "If you need me, tomorrow I'll be at the church early!"

Kelly leaves the dinner table and enters the lounge to check in on Michael. Seeing his fury, she asks, "Babe, what is it?"

When Kelly sees what is on the news, she's horrified. She grabs the control from Michael's hand and turns the TV off, then she tries to comfort him. "Babe, there's nothing you could have done!"

Michael clenches both his fists and shuts his eyes. "I could have done something!" he whispered to his wife. "Father Brian encouraged me to do a patrol tonight, to scope out what we don't know, but I didn't listen and now they're dead!"

"Babe!" Kelly said as she sits them both down. "I hate to say it, but I'm glad you didn't go out!"

"What?!" Michael barks as he looks at his wife.

"I'm sorry for being selfish, but I don't want you to end up like them! This is getting too real, too fast!" Kelly cries.

"I need to do something; I can't hide away from this!" Michael declares.

"NO!" Kelly shouts.

"Hun, it's Christmas tomorrow," Michael replies calmly. "The world can't wake up in terror. I need to show my presence."

"NO!" she shakes her head while all three kids peep in from the lounge entrance.

"What's going on?" Emma asks as she stands with her two little brothers hugging her legs.

"The news…" Michael begins to tell the kids, but Kelly interjects.,

"Don't!"

"They must know," Michael says as he kisses his wife on the forehead and rises to his feet "The news said there were two more angels."

"What? Really?" Emma cries excitedly.

"Yes, but they were badly hurt," Michael replies.

"Oh," Emma's smile disappears. "Are they going to be okay?"

Michael shakes his head in sorrow.

"Can we see the news?" Emma asks.

"NO!" Kelly said in a firm voice.

"Oh, come on, I'm just going to look it up on my phone."

"Give me your phone," Kelly commands.

"Mum, please!" Emma protests.

"Okay, I'll check to see if it's okay to look," Michael said as he reaches for his phone and checks social media. Then he tells Kelly, "Okay, they've taken them both down!"

"Fine!" Kelly says exhaustedly.

"Okay, you can watch, but only for a little while," Michael says as he reaches for the remote and turns the TV back on.

"It's unfortunate that the world has been gifted these heroes only to have them ripped away from us," the news reporter says

solemnly as the angels lay lifelessly on the pavement with their wings wrapped over them. Police officers, the ambulance crew and even bystanders watch and weep from the sidelines.

"That's sad," Hudson says.

"Okay, that's enough," Kelly declares as she turns the TV off again.

Michael says in a firm manner, "Hun, I must GO!"

"Where?" all the kids ask.

"THERE!" Michael answers, pointing towards the television.

"HUH?" they all reply in a confused way.

Kelly takes a deep sigh as she stands and walks over to the Christmas tree. "You might as well have an early Christmas present," she says as she reaches for a gift. "Here," she said and hands it to her husband.

"Well, go and try it on!" she adds, pointing towards their bedroom. Michael smiles as he gives her a kiss on the cheek and walks off to the bedroom with the present.

"Mum! What's going on? Emma asks.

"Just wait and see!"

Michael walks in with a suit on. It is a knee length peacoat with matching pants finished with a long collar that reaches his nose for identity concealment. The colour is gunmetal grey.

"Whoa! Dad, you look awesome!" Hudson exclaims.

"Looks good, Hun!" Michael says as he turns around.

"Looking good, babe!" Kelly replies

"What are these?" Isaiah asks, pointed towards the two cuts on the back of his peacoat.

"Well, I'll show you," Michael said as he looks over at his wife for approval. Kelly gives him a nod. The kids all sit with their mother on the sofa and wait in anticipation. Michael stands in front of them and slowly allows his wings to emerge from the cuts on his new peacoat.

"Oh my God!" both boys yell and jump about.

"YOU'RE HIM?" Emma exclaims. "The one on the news?"

"Yes!" Michael replies.

"Dad! You're, like, a hero."

"Well, if I am I need to go to the city! Right now!"

"Is it safe for you to go there? Emma asks.

"I don't know, Hun."

"Will you be back?"

"I will always come back."

"Okay, well then I think it's important you go," Emma replies, seeming older than her years.

"WHAT!" Kelly protests.

"Think about it, Mum! The world is in shock right now. We've lost two angels. The world is now thinking: Where are the others? Are there any others? I know that's what I'm thinking!"

Kelly ponders her daughter's words, then she stands up and faces her husband. "That is all you're doing, Michael! Just showing up, no dangerous stuff! I mean it!"

"Yes, Hun! Michael replies before they kiss, then he heads to the front door.

"You not taking the car?" Kelly asks.

"I think I might stretch my wings!" he replies with a smile before opening the door, "I won't be too long, I promise!" he reassures his family, then he steps outside and extends his wings to their full span.

"Bye!" Raising both his hands and his wings upright, he propels himself into the air leaving behind him a gust of wind.

"Wow! That was so cool!" Isaiah says to Hudson while Kelly and Emma worry in silence. They both rush back to the lounge and turn on the TV to be kept updated.

***

"Okay, come on, Michael!" he whispers to himself. "Let's get there quickly! Use your muscles!"

He winces as he propels his wings strongly and quickly through the air. He gets to the city in no time at all.

"Are we ready now?" Sergeant Mourning yells at the crime scene crew that are taking photos of the deceased.

"We're good here!" one of the crime scene techs says as he gives the Sergeant the thumbs up.

"Okay, go ahead!" Sergeant Mourning tells the ambulance crew, giving them the clear to remove the angel's bodies. A sudden gust of wind comes from out of nowhere and the ominous sound of wings flapping can be heard above, like the sail on a boat caught in the wind. Everyone tries to get a glimpse of what it is, but they lose sight of it. The news reporter tries to investigate but to no avail.

"What was that?" Sergeant Mourning yells.

"I don't know, sir," Constable Alonzo replies, then he asks his colleagues, "Did anyone get a look?"

"NO!" they chorus back.

"Are you ready?" the news reporter shouts at the cameraman.

"Almost!" he replies as he fumbles with the camera equipment.

"Well, HURRY UP!"

"Yes, yes!" the cameraman sighs in response, then he hoists the camera onto his shoulders and points it at the female reporter. "Okay, I'm ready!"

The cameraman holds up three fingers in the air for the reporter to see and counts down to one.

"In breaking news," the reporter begins, "Something is hovering over us here in the city square. We heard what sounded like the flapping or large wings, but it seems to have ceased for now."

"Mum! Mum! Dad is on the news!" Emma shouts out, glued to the TV.

"Okay, coming!" Kelly calls as she rushes back into the lounge with a bowl of ice cream for them both.

"We are unsure if it's safe or—"

The news reporter is interrupted when a bystander points towards one of the taller buildings and shouts, "LOOK! UP THERE!"

Michael is on his haunches looking on with his wings spread out, unaware that his eyes are glowing white in the darkness. He slowly stands upright, glaring down at them all, allowing the cameraman to get a good view of him.

"Sweet Mary!" Sergeant Mourning whispers as he gazes up at Michael in complete awe. The news reporter is so taken aback by Michael that she forgets to conclude her report.

"That camera angle makes your father look a lot taller, doesn't it?" Kelly comments to her daughter.

The figure hiding in the darkness also looks up at Michael. Spreading their own wings they flew up towards him. He could hear the wings of another angel flapping nearby, but before he had the chance to look the angel landed next to him and stood by him proudly.

"Whoa!" Emma cries out, "Mum, check it out! Another angel has showed up!"

"Thank God!" Kelly says. She was relieved that her husband now had backup.

"Ahem!" the cameraman coughs, trying to regain the news reporter's attention.

"Sorry folks, I'm a little distracted; now there are two angels watching over us here in the city."

The moment the news reporter finished her report, another angel landed next to Michael, making it three. The crowd could no longer contain their excitement and cheered. Michael, being the larger Angel of the three, turns around and gets ready to fly.

"Please come with me! We need to talk."

The two angels nod in agreement and wait for him to lead the way. Michael jumps off the roof of the building and flies off. The other two follow swiftly behind, whilst below the crowd cheers them on and say their goodbyes.

"There you have it, folks. While we mourn the two Angels we've lost, we have gained three more. The big question now is are there any more of them?"

"Wow! Do you think there are more, Mum?" Emma asks.

"I hope so, Honey" Kelly replies, "I hope so."

Chapter 20

City of Angels

Michael picks another roof top to land on, only this time the building is a little taller, making it harder for anyone to see them. Michael lands and retracts his wings, as do his companions. Michael turns around to face the other two angels. One is male, and his wings match his earth brown hair. The other is a female with dark blonde wings with a streak of purple just like her hair. Both appear far too young for such big responsibilities.

"Are you even out of your teens?" Michael asks with a grin.

"My name is Quinn," the young man replies, "and I'm twenty-five."

Quinn seems full of life and exudes self-confidence.

"And you…wait, I know you," Michael tells the female angel, looking at her closely

"Yes, I was the one that was on the news the other night saving those two cars from crashing on the freeway."

"No! I've seen you somewhere else," Michael says, studying her, trying to figure it out.

"You, um, stood up for me against my ex on the train, remember?"

Michael recalls the memory of her abuse on the train. He disarmed her attacker and took away his knife. "I hope he didn't come back into your life?"

"He tried to call once or twice, but what you did that day changed my life; I didn't know strangers like you existed. Everyone always looked away and minded their own business, so I always felt alone when I faced his abuse. That is until YOU came along. That's why I'll follow you anywhere." Holding out her hand she said, "My name is Hannah, and I'm twenty-four."

"Michael," he says as he shakes her hand and then Quinn's, "and I'm not telling either of you my age." They laugh, then Michael asks, "So, have you met the others?"

"There's more?" Quinn replies, amazed.

"There should be seven in total."

"WHOA! Seven?" Quinn exclaims, his eyes wide.

"Why seven?" Hannah asks, "how do you know that?"

"Because there were—or are—seven archangels," Michael replies. "The night of the storm, you were struck by lightning, right? That's how we've inherited these gifts from God."

"How did you know that I was struck by lightning?" Hannah asks.

"Because I was too!" Michael replies. "I believe we all were. That;s God's twisted way of passing on this gift. The gifts of his strongest angels, the archangels,"

Quinn raised his hand as if in school.

"Yes, Quinn?"

"What are archangels? And how do you know it was God that passed these gifts on to us? And why do you think He passed them onto us?"

Michael shakes his head. "Do either of you know about angels?" Michael asks.

"Nope!"

"Okay," Michael sighs. "This is a crash-course. There are guardian angels: ones that watch over us. Then there are the archangels: these angels are the soldier angels and are a lot stronger than your normal angels. There were seven of these archangels and their names were Gabriel, Raphael, Uriel, Selaphiel, Raguel and Barachiel."

Quinn is counting on his fingers. "Hold up, that was six angels!"

"The last angel was Michael."

"Er, is he like related to you?" Quinn asks.

"NO! It just means we take after these archangels. Maybe I take after Michael. I don't know; I'm learning as I go."

"I think I take after Uriel," Hannah says with a smile. "I like that name!"

"Well, whichever badass archangel there is, I must take after him!" Quinn declares while both Hannah and Michael roll their eyes.

"Anyway," Michael tries to change the subject, "I spoke with someone the other night who I think may be God."

"WHAT?" Hannah and Quinn cry, then the latter asks, "What did he say? NO! What did he look like?"

"He told me something was coming, but He didn't say what or when, only that something was coming."

Hannah observes Michael's body language then she prompts, "What is it? There's more, isn't there?"

"I think that something is already here." Michael replies grimly. "The Pope dying was suspicious enough, but with two angels also dying…? It proves that something wicked is already here."

"So, what now?" Quinn asks.

"Now we must be vigilant!" Michael replies. "We need to watch each other's backs and not to do anything silly."

"Okay. How do we contact each other, Michael? Hannah asks.

"Through prayer."

"Through what?" Quinn replies.

"I have a priest friend in the suburb where I live. He prayed to me and I heard him in my head," Michael explains, only vaguely aware of how ludicrous it sounds.

"How do we do that?" Quinn asks excitedly.

Michael spreads out his wings and flies high into the air until he was just a speck. "Hannah, Quinn, please hear my prayer!" he whispers whilst hovering above them.

"I can hear him!" Quinn says, while Hannah closes her eyes and smiles.

"If you both can hear me, join me up here!"

They both spread out their wings and flew up towards Michael.

"That was a cool trick!" Quinn tells him.

"Yeah!" Hannah agrees.

"Okay, so we know how to contact one another," Michael tells them. "It works both ways as well. If

anything happens, let the others know. And remember—
no hero stuff!"

"Hey, why are you looking at me?!" " Quinn replies,
but with a smile.

Michael looks at Hannah and says in a fatherly tone,
"If you need anything, you let me know."

"Yes, DAD!" Hannah jokes with Michael who smirks
back at her. She grins, "Wow, you smiled!"

"No, I didn't!" Michael says firmly.

"Yes, you did! I saw it!" Quinn adds.

Trying to hold back a smile, Michael says, "Okay, now
get out of here you two!"

Quinn and Hannah give Michael a wave before tilting
their wings and speeding off, leaving a gust of wind
behind them. As Michael watches them both fly away, he
whispers to himself, "Kids!" Tilting his body on a slight
angle, he positions his wings and surges forward.

Constable Sacks checks the church near Michael's
home, but the doors are locked. As she heads back
towards her car she sees Michael up in the sky. She hops
into her car, guns the engine and skids out of the church
parking lot to give chase.

"What luck!" she mutters under her breath as she tails
Michael, then she sees him slowing down and descending
only a street away.

"He lives close by?" Megan wonders aloud, then she
pulls over her car on a nearby street and sees Michael land
in the park outside his home. Megan turns her headlights
off and watches as Michael walks out of the park. She
ducks her head low into the front passenger seat of her

car, then she slowly raises her head up and over the dashboard and sees Michael on the phone talking to someone. The garage door of a house opens, and he walks in and greets a woman with a hug.

"So glad it went well," Kelly tells Michael upon his return, "and that you're safe."

"I told you it was going to be okay," he gives her a kiss, then he asks, "are the kids awake?"

"No! They went to bed. Emma stayed up with me until it was all over. She crashed around twenty minutes ago."

"We better get to bed as well. Big day tomorrow—Christmas!" he says with a smile.

"Don't remind me," she groans, then they head into the house and close the garage.

From the dark park across the road, Megan grins and her eyes glow a dull yellow. "Gotcha!" she whispers, before starting her car and driving off.

Chapter 21

The Calm Before The Storm

Morning breaks and everyone wakes to embrace the new day. Michael is disturbed from his sleep as two excited little boys come racing into the bedroom and jump on the bed. Kelly is already up and in the kitchen cooking Christmas breakfast.

"Uh, what do you two want?" Michael murmured into his pillow.

"We want you to get up, Dad!" Hudson said.

"Yeah, so we can open our presents!" Isaiah adds.

"Argh! Okay, I'm getting up."

"YAY!" both boys yell before rushing out of their parent's bedroom.

Michael hops out of bed goes to the bathroom to freshen up, then he makes his way to the loudest part of the house, the lounge room, where the Christmas tree is.

Michael greets Kelly with a kiss. "Merry Christmas, hun!"

"Merry Christmas, babe!" Kelly replied.

"Did you want coffee? Michael asks her.

"Yes please!"

Michael turns on their coffee machine and empties a bag coffee beans into it, then he yells out, "Boys, have you started to open your presents?"

"No, not yet, Dad!" Hudson replies.

"Why?"

"We're organising our presents first to see how much we have!"

Kelly laughs when Michael slightly cringes, and she whispers, "Don't worry, they have the same number of presents, I made sure!"

"Oh, thank God!"

"No, thank your wife."

"Thanks, hun!" Michael says as he pecks Kelly on the cheek.

"We have eight presents each!" Hudson cries.

"Okay, now can we open them?" Isaiah asks his brother.

"Yes!"

"Hang on!" Kelly says. "Is Emma still asleep?"

"Yeah," Hudson replies.

"Hmm, okay you can start opening your presents. We'll be waiting forever for that kid to wake," Kelly says, shaking her head.

The boys pick the biggest presents first and work their way down to the smallest. Kelly places breakfast on the table, then she watches her husband place her coffee on the kitchen bench. She reaches for it, but he says, "Hang on, I'm not done!"

He shakes chocolate powder over the surface of Kelly's coffee completing his work of art. "There we are!"

"Thank you. Where's yours?"

"We ran out of coffee beans," Michael informs her.

"Oh, Babe, you should have told me! This should have been your coffee. You need it more than I do after the big night you had!"

"That's why I didn't tell you," Michael replies. "I'm good. I'll just have juice."

They watch the kids open their presents as they enjoy their breakfast, then Kelly asks her husband, "Do we dare turn on the TV?"

"Maybe after breakfast," Michael replies. "Too early for the news."

'Dear Michael and Quinn, please hear my Prayer,' Michael suddenly hears Hannah's voice say in his head. He closes his eyes and listens, afraid that something is wrong.

'Merry Christmas to you and your families'

Michael lets out a big sigh of relief.

'Merry Christmas!' Quinn replies.

'Merry Christmas, you two,' Michael tells them with a smile. *'And stay safe!'*

'Why do I think that last part was meant for me?' Quinn jokes.

Michael laughed. *'Very funny! Now go away and enjoy your day!'*

He opens his eyes to find Kelly watching him.

"Who was that?"

"The two new recruits, Hannah and Quinn. They wished us a Merry Christmas."

"Aww, that was nice of them!"

"Yeah, they are good kids!" Michael says with a smile.

"Maybe you should see your priest friend later today," Kelly suggests.

"Yeah, I was thinking of catching up with Father Brian after morning mass."

"Okay, I'll take the kids to Mum and Dad's place when you go."

***

Constable Sacks treads confidently through stinking sewer water at knee height in the dark, dank tunnel. Moans and growls echo through the maze of tunnels, scaring away anyone that gets near.

"Master, I have news!" Megan yells as she reaches her destination.

"It better be good!" a terrifying voice growls from one of the wider tunnels, then the huge creature emerges and demands, "Well? What is it?"

"I know who the BIG angel is and where he lives…and more importantly, where his family lives!" Megan says.

"HA-HA-HA-HA! First we discover there are three angels and now the BIG one has a family! Oh, this is too easy!" The creature laughs some more, then he rallies his troops, shaking them one by one as he walks through the horde. "Tomorrow we attack!"

In the presbytery, Father Brian and Michael sit down to discuss the newcomers.

"Here you go!" the priest said as he hands Michael a cup of coffee.

"Thank you, Father."

"So, these two new angels," Father Brian begins as he sits opposite his guest. "Tell me about them!"

"One is male, the other is female. Both are young and they don't seem particularly combat ready!"

"Well, that's where you come in, Michael," Father Brian replies.

"It's too much of a job! The fight that is yet to come, I feel…" Michael finds it hard to find the words. He places his coffee down on the table and says, "They shouldn't have to worry about it. They should be out dating or shopping or thinking about their future, not fighting some supernatural war!"

Father Brian sits up a little taller. . "I'm not afraid for their safety, because they have you."

Michael shrugs off the vote of confidence. "You have too much faith in me, Father."

"And you have too much humility," Father Brian counters with a smile, then they both sit back and sip from their cups. "I don't suppose you know what killed those two angels?"

Michael shook his head. "No. I couldn't see anything abnormal when we arrived, but I did notice that the bodies of the angels had been pierced with something."

"I thought that angels were almost indestructible," Father Brian ponders.

"Yeah, so did I," Michael mutters. "When I spoke with God, he told me I should be pretty durable and that nothing made by human hands can hurt me. Until we know what this supernatural weapon is and who wields it, we angels need to be vigilant and not do things alone."

"Right, well that's the next item on your 'TO DO' list," Father Brian says. "Let the others know."

Michael gives him a nod.

"This is why I like Christmas; the peace it brings," Father Brian says cheerfully.

"That's what scares me, the peace after that horrific event last night!" Michael confides.

Father Brian gives Michael a gentle smile and sips his coffee, saying "enjoy the peace while it lasts.".

Chapter 22

A Hero's Worth

A small skeleton staff operates the police station during the festive season. Constable Alonzo Verra and his partner Constable Julie Simmons sit and man the silent phones.

"Okay, remind me why did we volunteer to be the skeleton staff this year?" Julie asks.

"Because of the bonus pay for working during the festive season," Constable Alonzo replied.

"Right!" Julie says as she swivels on her chair, bored.

"Look at it from this angle, Julie. We're paid a bonus for working on Christmas Day for doing practically nothing. It's dead in here! Nothing happens on Christmas Day!"

One of the phones begins to ring.

"You jinxed us!" Julie tells him, then she rushes over to the front desk to answer the phone.

"Hello, Constable—" Julie begins, but is immediately cut off by the caller. "Okay, slow down! Well, have you tried calling a plumber? That doesn't fall under police duty Ma'am! Okay, I tell you what—if the noise is still happening after lunch, give us a call back. You're welcome, bye, Ma'am!"

Julie hangs up the phone and sighs.

"What was that about?" Constable Alonzo asked.

"That was a Miss Joan. Apparently, she's hearing some strange growling noises coming from her sink."

"That's a weird one."

"Ya think?" Julie replies, then she asks, "So, what are we doing for lunch?"

"Is anything actually open?"

"You could do a drive by of the takeaway places while I woman the fort," Julie suggests.

"Why me?"

"We're here because of you!"

"Hmm," Constable Alonzo replied as he grabbed his police jacket.

"Thank you!" Julie yells out as he leaves the station.

Constable Alonzo was having no luck with any of the usual takeaway places, all of them were closed. Seeing a petrol station, he looks at his fuel gauge and mutters to himself, "better fuel up."

He parks at the fuel station and begins to fill up his vehicle, contemplating the last few days and how odd they had been, especially the deaths of the two angels. The main reason he decided to take the holiday shift was he felt he owed it to the angels to keep working whilst everyone else was not.

"Whoops!" he says as the fuel nearly spills over, then he hangs up the nozzle of the bowser and heads into the station to pay. Fortunate for him the fuel station has a range of hot food in the bain-marie. "Can I get the two hamburgers, one with egg and the other without?" he says to the service attendant. "Oh, and the fuel on bowser four."

He pays and as he makes his way to his vehicle he notices a female driver in a white van and is stunned to recognise her as the missing officer, Constable Megan Sacks. He quickly rushes to his car and gives chase as the van drives off.

"Constable Alonzo to dispatch, come in dispatch!" he frantically calls the station on his radio.

"This is dispatch!" Constable Julie replies. "What's happening?"

"I've located Constable Sacks and I'm in pursuit."

"Constable Megan Sacks?" Julie exclaims.

"Yes. She's driving a white hire van, registration 1WHT-112. I'm going to follow her and see where she takes me. I just need you to be on standby for when I call in the location!"

"Will do!" Julie replies, then she warns him, "Just don't do anything silly."

"I won't!" he replies.

Julie patiently waits by the dispatch radio, hoping to hear back from her partner, then the phone rings, much to her annoyance.

"Argh! Why now? Hello? Listen Miss Joan, I understand that I told you to call back if the noises persist but now is not a great time. I will call you back in ten minutes, okay?” As Julie hangs up the phone someone enters the station.

“Everything okay here?” a familiar voice asks.

Julie jumps, then she turns around and sees Sergeant Andrew Mourning.

“Sarge!” she replies. “Sorry, I’m little on edge at the moment. Constable Alonzo is in pursuit of Constable Megan Sacks.”

“WHAT?” the sergeant exclaims, “Why wasn’t I informed, constable?”

“It has only just happened, sir.”

“Tell me exactly what occurred.”

“Well, Constable Alonzo went out to get lunch for us, then around twenty minutes later he calls in saying that he saw Constable Sacks driving a white van and that he was going to pursue her and will call back shortly.”

“Okay, we’ll wait to hear from him.”

A quarter of an hour later, Constable Alonzo calls in and is surprised when Sergeant Mourning answers instead of Julie.

“What’s the situation, Constable Alonzo?”

“Sir, I have pursued Constable Sacks to the Great Eastern overpass just outside the city. She drove to an entrance of a tunnel and I plan to pursue her on foot—"

“That is a negative. You do not have permission to pursue, do you copy, Constable?” When he doesn’t reply, Sergeant Mourning shouts, “Constable Alonzo!”

“I have to do this, Sergeant!” he replies.

“No! Do not pursue, that is an order!” Sergeant Mourning continues to shout while Julie looks on with concern.

"I REPEAT, DO NOT PURSUE! CONSTABLE ALONZO, COME IN!"

He doesn't get a response, much to Julie's horror.

"DAMN IT!" Sergeant Mourning roars in frustration as he throws down the radio handset, then he looks at Julie and commands, "You stay here while I go find Constable Alonzo."

"Yes, sir," Julie replies as she wipes a tear away from her face and hopes to hear from her partner again.

Sergeant Mourning grabs his coat and car keys and rushes towards a police vehicle. He turns on the sirens and speeds out of the station parking lot while shouting to himself, "Alonzo, you fool, what are you doing?"

Constable Alonzo has parked his car a street away from the tunnel entrance and watches Constable Sacks collect some belongings from the van and leave it at the entrance.

Constable Alonzo parks behind it and turns his vehicle beacon on before he leaves the car. He takes his gun out of the holster and cautiously approaches the van. He peeks through the back windscreen and sees nothing. Pointing his gun downwards, he creeps towards the passenger door of the van. He raises his gun but there is no one inside.

"Okay," he sighs, then he looks at the dark tunnel and steels himself to walk into it. He closes his eyes and draws in a deep breath, then he opens his eyes and exhales slowly. He reaches for his flashlight and points it ahead of him along with his gun as he cautiously enters the tunnel. The flashlight cannot penetrate the darkness, so he is still unable to see what's ahead of him. Finally, the flashlight illuminates a T-junction.

"Damn it!" he whispered to himself. "Do I go left or right? Left it is," he decides, then he takes a few steps down the left tunnel before removing his police jacket and leaving it on the ground to indicate which direction he headed in.

Treading through the tunnel with great stealth, Constable Alonzo tries his best not to cause a commotion, especially with the sewerage water at his feet.

The smell starts to get to him as he walks deeper into the tunnel. Suddenly he begins to hear eerie groaning noises ahead of him. He raises his gun as he walks steadily towards the noises. He can see a light ahead of him, which means the tunnel does have an exit. However, the noises seem to be getting louder and more disturbing as he approaches the light.

"Just a few more steps!" he mutters to himself, as he inches closer and closer to the edge of the exit, hiding himself as best he can in the shadows of the tunnel. He has a quick scan of the perimeter, then he sees a horde of rabid humans behaving erratically. They crash and bump into each other; some seem to be fighting each other. Freaked out by what he is seeing, Constable Alonzo grabs his two-way radio from his utility waist belt, lowers the volume and pushes the talk button.

"Dispatch, come in. This is Constable Alonzo. Over!" he whispers.

Silence. He tries again.

"Dispatch, come in, this is Constable Alonzo. We have a situation here. Over!"

"What situation?" says a female voice behind him.

Spooked, Constable Alonzo spins around quickly, but Constable Sacks knocks him out with her gun.

"Bring him!" she commands one of the creatures by her side. "We'll see what the boss has to say."

***

"What's going on?" Hannah wonders when she hears sirens outside her third-floor apartment. She looks out the window and sees a police car racing at full speed with lights flashing. Hannah contemplates whether or not she should follow.

"Eh, what's the worst that could happen?" she tells herself. "I'll call the others if it's serious!"

Hannah quickly puts on casual denim pants and a white thin mesh hooded jumper over her white tank top. She hops into the elevator and heads to the top of the ten-storey building. The other buildings block her view, so she kneels on the roof and listens to the sirens to try to pinpoint its location. She realises the police vehicle is heading towards the Great Eastern overpass.

"Okay, Hannah, nothing too brave. Just a little recon job and back again."

She runs towards the edge of the roof and jumps off. Her wings spread out and she glides away towards the sirens.

Sergeant Mourning slows down, trying to locate Constable Alonzo's vehicle. He recalls that he mentioned a tunnel near the overpass bridge, so he drives off the road and heads down towards a park. He looks to his right and sees Constable Alonzo's vehicle at the entrance of the tunnel. Grabbing his radio he turns it on and reports, "Dispatch, this is Sergeant Mourning! Come in!"

"This is dispatch!" Constable Julie replied. "What's happening, sir?"

"I've found Constable Alonzo's vehicle, but it seems to be empty. I'm going to check it out and will report back ASAP."

"Copy that, sir."

Sergeant Mourning exits his vehicle and approaches Constable Alonzo's car which is empty. He unholsters his gun and approaches the white van on the driver side of the vehicle.

He flings opens the door, announcing himself as police as he does so, and points his gun: no one is in sight. The sergeant looks at the dark tunnel and contemplates whether he should go in without backup. He then returns to Constable Alonzo's vehicle and picks up the radio.

"Dispatch, its Sergeant Mourning. Come in!"

"This is dispatch. Go ahead, sir." Constable Julie replied.

"Constable Alonzo isn't anywhere in sight and neither is Constable Sacks. I think he's pursued her into a nearby tunnel. I need to go in after him as he has no back up."

Julie wants to tell the sergeant it is too dangerous, but if her partner was alone in that tunnel he may need assistance.

"Dispatch? Are you there? Come in!"

"Dispatch here, copy that, sir!" Constable Julie replied, then as she turns off the radio she breaks down, her sobs echoing through the empty police station.

Sergeant Mourning heads into the tunnel with haste, his mind racing, and hopes that his constable is still in one piece. When he sees the T-junction he swears under his breath, then he sees Constable Alonzo's police jacket lying near the entrance of the left tunnel.

"Shit!" he whispers to himself, fearing the worst. Without a care for his own safety he runs down the tunnel, then he hears horrific growling sounds echoing hauntingly throughout the tunnel system.

Spooked, Sergeant Mourning wonders, "What the hell is that?"

His fears for Constable Alonzo's safety increase as he heads quickly down the tunnel. Seeing some light at the end, he urges himself to head towards it. As he approaches the light the growling noises grow even louder, but this doesn't deter him; instead it has the opposite effect.

"Please be okay!" he mutters under his breath, "Please be okay!"

He slowly approaches the end of tunnel and just before the exit sees a pit the size of a basketball court filled with people. This pit has five other tunnels leading out from it and the occupants look ghastly; their flesh is rotten and the smell is horrific. The sergeant gags and tries not to vomit. The zombie-like figures seem to be unaware of their surroundings. Sergeant Mourning tries to investigate without leaving the tunnel he's in, then he spots Constable Sacks walking with a creature, the sight of which shook the sergeant to his core.

"Get everyone into position and be ready," the creature tells Constable Sacks, "we attack tomorrow at dusk."

"What in God's name is *that?*" Sergeant Mourning whispers to himself.

Suddenly the creature's head snaps to the side, his grotesque ears pricked: he had heard the officer's whisper and turns his head towards the tunnel in which the sergeant is hiding.

"Get him!" it shrieks, pointing in his direction.

"Shit!" Sergeant Mourning says, then he turned and ran as fast as he could back towards the way he came in. He could hear snarling and growling behind him, the echoing of the tunnel made it sound as though they were close behind him.

"Shit, shit, shit!" he swears while trying to find the T-junction leading to the exit. When he finds it he makes a right turn and sprints towards the light at the opening of the tunnel. He clamps his eyes shut as he surges towards it, praying he will make it.

"Hello?" a female voice calls.

Sergeant Mourning opens his eyes again and gasps when he sees a winged figure standing at the entrance of the tunnel.

"HELP!" he yelled, "HELP ME! I'M IN HERE!"

"I'm coming!" Hannah shouts back, running into the tunnel. Seeing the sergeant frantically running for his life, she holds out her hand to him.

"Quick!" she shouts.

Sergeant Mourning can see an angel calling to him, her body framed with sunlight; she is holding out her hand

and her wings are open to their majestic full span. It would be a pretty sight if not for the zombie-like humans chasing him on all fours.

Hannah is shocked when she sees these terrifying creatures, but she knows she has to be strong. She grasps Sergeant Mourning's hands, then holding him close she whispers into his ear, "It's okay. The big angel's name is Michael. Pray to him and he will answer your prayer."

Hannah then pushes him out of the tunnel and blocks it off with her wings so the monsters can't escape.

"NOOOO!" Sergeant Mourning shouts as he falls to the ground. He looks over his shoulder and sees Hannah holding the creatures back. They begin to gnaw on her shoulders and wings, but still, she stands strong.

"Go!" she cries out in pain. "And remember what I said!"

He picks himself up and runs towards his car, then as he drives out of the park, throwing one last glance over his shoulder at Hannah. Unable to stand, she has fallen to her knees, and he watches in horror as she is dragged into the tunnel.

Sergeant Mourning cries out in rage and punches his steering wheel repeatedly to vent his fury and his grief, then he lets his tears fall as he speeds back to the police station. He drives his car right up to the main door, then he leaps out of the vehicle, runs into the station and crashes into the front desk, nearly toppling it over

"JULIE!" he yells. "WHERE ARE YOU?"

"Here, Sergeant!" Julie replies. She is standing to his right by the dispatch radio.

"GET EVERY WEAPON WE HAVE IN THE ARMOURY AND POOL THEM HERE!" he yells, pointing to the front desk, which is the biggest desk in the station.

Seeing his panic, Julie asks, "What's going on, sir?"

"I'll explain later! Just do this for me while I recall every officer we have!"

Constable Julie rushes to the armoury while Sergeant Mourning locks himself away in his office and picks up his phone.

Chapter 23

The Prayer

Michael and his family have been enjoying a Christmas picnic at their local park. When the sun begins to set, he starts to pack the car while the kids play in the playground.

"Boys, we're leaving in ten!" Michael shouts out to his sons, but they don't respond. "I don't think they heard me."

"All kids have selective hearing," Kelly jokes.

"Well, whether they heard me or not, we're going in ten minutes," Michael replied as he picked up the boys' shoes and placed them in the car.

Back at the police station, cars are beginning to fill up the parking lot. A handful of officers are inside talking to each other. Constable Julie taps on the glass door of Sergeant Mourning's office.

"One minute!" he yells out to her and she gives him a thumbs up.

Sergeant Mourning places the palms of his hands together and closes his eyes. "This feels weird," he whispers to himself, but he puts all his faith in his prayer, hoping to hear something, anything. *'Uh, Angel Michael please hear my prayer. Hello, Angel Michael? Are you there?'*

When he doesn't hear anything, he unclasps his hands, stands up and shakes his head, "I knew this wasn't going to work!"

'Who is this?' A voice suddenly replies.

Sergeant Mourning is stunned. Sitting back down, he presses his hands together again and replies, *'my name is Andrew Mourning. Sergeant Andrew Mourning.'*

'What do you want?'

'I would like to see you. I have news—'

'NO!' Michael rudely answers back.

'Please, sir, it's about the other angel – the girl.'

'Hannah?' Michael asks with concern. *'What about her?'*

'She, uh, um…'

'She what?' Michael asks impatiently.

'She … died.' Sergeant Mourning waits, but he hears no response. *'Angel Michael? Are you there?'*

'Where are you now, Sergeant?' Michael asks.

'I'm at the Police station. I'm going to lead an attack on the things that did this.'

Kelly is sitting in the park in a camping chair watching her husband when he suddenly falls to his knees. Shocked, she rushes to his aid.

"Michael! Are you okay?" she asks as she helps him up, then seeing that his face is filled with pain she asks, "What happened?"

"It's Hannah," Michael replies. "I think she's dead."

"Why do you think that?"

"Sergeant Mourning just told me something happened…"

"What else did he say?" Kelly asked.

"He wants to see me. He's at the police station."

"I think you should go, maybe take Quinn," Kelly suggests.

"Yeah!" Michael replies, "you okay with the kids?"

"Yeah, Mum and Dad are here so we'll be fine. We may stay a bit longer."

"Okay, I will see you tonight!" Michael says as he takes a step backwards. As his wings spread out his singlet rips off him.

"Damn it! I'm going to have no clothes left at this rate!"

"Go and get your outfit back home," Kelly suggests.

Michael gives her a kiss then he propels himself into the air and flies off. Kelly shields her eyes from the gust of wind his wings cause and whispers to herself, "You better come home"

"Quinn!" Michael says out loud, not bothering with the formalities of how a prayer should be said.

Michael? Is that you?

"Yes, it's me," Michael confirms. "I have news."

'About…?'

'It's Hannah.'

Hearing the sorrow in Michael's voice, Quinn asks with concern, *What about her?*

"I think she's been killed," Michael replies quickly.

What!' Quinn cries, shocked. *When? How?*

"I don't know. I'm heading to the police station to find out!"

"The police station?" Quinn asks.

"Yes. Sergeant Mourning told me the news using prayer," Michael tells him. "I guess Hannah told him how to do it."

Quinn's initial shock turns to anger. "ARE WE GOING TO GET THE PEOPLE THAT DID THIS?"

"We're sure as hell gonna try!" Michael assures him. "Meet me at the police station."

Sergeant Mourning leaves his office and assesses how many officers he has at his disposal. "Are they all here?" he asks Julie.

"Not all, sir. Many have gone on holidays with their families for the festive season."

"Okay, this is a good turnout," he said as he looks at everyone present, then they all gather around him.

"Why are we here Sarge?"

He quickly tells them that Constable Alonzo saw Constable Sacks and followed her into a tunnel under the Great Eastern Overpass.

"Concerned for Constable Alonzo's welfare, I went into this tunnel and found an infestation of zombie-like humans and a big ugly creature conveying information to Constable Sacks. I wouldn't have made it out of the tunnel if it wasn't for a brave angel called Hannah who sacrificed herself so that I may live," he concludes. He looks around at stunned faces. "I don't know what happened to Constable Alonzo, but I fear the worst."

There was shocked silence for a moment, the whole

group processing such weird news. Then an officer asks, "When you say 'zombie-like' what do you mean, sarge?"

"They were human, but not human at the same time!"

"Like possessed humans?" Constable Julie asks anxiously.

"I don't know; I honestly don't."

"How many of them were there, sir?"

"Too many to count," Sergeant Mourning replies with a grimace. "An army of them, including that larger creature."

"How are thirty police officers supposed to defeat an undead army?" one of the louder officers asks, then they all began to mutter amongst themselves.

"I'm sorry, sir, but I have a family to think of."

"So do I!" others join in and begin to head for the front door, but before they have a chance to leave Michael and Quinn land heavily in the carpark outside the police station.

"WHAT THE HELL?"

"Oh, my God!"

"I've called for reinforcements!" Sergeant Mourning tells them as he heads outside; the rest of the officers follow him. The darkness of the night makes the angels look ominous, but Sergeant Mourning isn't afraid when he approaches them.

"I'm relieved you made it, both of you! I can't tell you how much it means to me to be in your presence. It's unfortunate we have to meet under these circumstances."

Quinn looks away, grief-stricken. Michael took a step forward into the light, revealing his identity, and Quinn follows his lead. All the officers gaze upon them in awe.

"What happened to Hannah, Sergeant Mourning?" Michael asks.

"She saved my life! While looking for a missing officer in the tunnel under the Great Eastern Overpass I found an army of creatures that looked human but weren't. When they chased me I thought I was going to die, but then she came," he said with a touch of sorrow in his voice. "Hannah stayed and blocked the entrance so that the creatures couldn't escape and they attacked her instead of me."

Quinn's wings droop and he looks at the ground. Michael places a hand on his shoulder for comfort. Quinn walks back into the shadows to try and hide his emotion, but as his fluorescent angel's tears glow a bright trail down his cheeks in the darkness.

"I'm sorry," Sergeant Mourning apologises.

Michael also sheds a tear for Hannah, but his expression doesn't change. "Thank you, Sergeant. We'll take it from here."

"You need us."

"No!" Michael replies firmly. "You'll just get in the way."

"But you don't know where it is?"

"You said the Great Eastern Overpass. I know the tunnel," Michael says, then he turns to Quinn and pats him on the shoulder. The pair of angels fly off leaving behind a gust of wind.

"Come on, grab your weapons and let's go!" Sergeant Mourning yells as he rallies his own troops. "They're going to need us, no matter what they say."

Chapter 24

The Horseman's Test

Michael and Quinn fly as fast as they can to the location. There is no conversation between them; both are ready for whatever comes at them tonight.

"There!" Michael says, pointing down at a police vehicle with its lights still on outside a large tunnel, a white van in front of it. "That's the tunnel!"

They both land, then Michael looks at the entrance.

"We're going in?" Quinn asks.

"Yes, but you follow behind and I want total silence from here on, okay?"

Quinn nods back in agreement.

At the entrance of the tunnel, they notice lots of blood and dishevelled feathers from Hannah. Quinn screws up his face and grits his teeth in anger. Michael gives him a comforting pat on his shoulder, then they follow the trail of blood and feathers to a T-junction. The trail leads them to the left tunnel where they also see Constable Alonzo's police jacket. They look at each other and nod, knowing they're close, then a scream echoes through the tunnels.

"Hannah!" Quinn gasps as he pushes his way past Michael.

"Quinn! No!" Michael shouts, but Quinn doesn't listen and Michael chases after him.

Moonlight illuminates the pit area. Quinn approaches the exit and finds twenty human-like figures.

"Oh, that smell!" Quinn says, covering his mouth and nose.

Michael catches up to Quinn and gasps when he sees what has captured his friend's attention.

"What are they, Michael?" Quinn whispers.

"I don't know."

"They don't seem to know we're here," Quinn observes.

"Yeah, they just walk aimlessly and bump into each other like zombies!" Michael says, watching them intently.

"Are they zombies?" Quinn asks.

"They can't be zombies; they're not real!"

"I didn't think that angels were real either, but here we are!" Quinn points out.

"True!" Michael concedes as he continues to observe these strange humans. Quinn notices that one of them is gnawing away at something.

"What is that?" he asks as he steps out of the tunnel, exposing himself in order to get a better view. He is infuriated when he sees one of the creatures is gnawing on one of Hannah's wings.

"Quinn, wait!" Michael hisses, but it is too late—the strange humans all go insane and charge for them both.

"COME ON!" Quinn yells at them, eager for a fight.

Michael joins him. Every blow from the two angels was so powerful that whenever they hit one of the rotten humans a part of their anatomy was severed from their body. They were no match for two enraged angels who made short work of them all.

"That was a little too easy," Quinn says as he lifts up Hannah's severed wing and holds it tight.

"Yes, it was!" Michael agrees. "Let's go!"

The angels were unaware of another presence; someone or something had watched them battle in the moonlit sewer.

As Michael and Quinn walked out of the tunnel, they hear sirens and see flashing lights as police vehicles pull into the nearby park. Sergeant Mourning gets out of his car and sees the two angels have spots of blood on them. The younger one is holding a severed angel wing.

"What happened?"

"They attacked us; we had to defend ourselves," Michael replies, "there weren't many of them. Maybe twenty."

Sergeant Mourning is sceptical and asks, did you get the big guy?"

"There was no big guy," Michael replies.

"No! WAIT!" Sergeant Mourning cries, grabbing hold of Michael's arm as he turns to leave. "The big guy said they would attack tomorrow at DUSK! I think something bigger is going on."

"We'll be watching, Sergeant," Michael assures him, then the angels walk over to the park and bury Hannah's wing in the ground.

"Bye, Hannah," Quinn whispers sadly, then he flies off with Michael.

"What do you think is going on?" Quinn asks.

"I don't know," Michael replies grimly, "but it looks as though it's just you and me, kid. So, no more heroics, okay?"

"I promise!" Quinn says.

"I'm going home. If I find out anything more, I'll contact, you!"

"Okay," Quinn says, giving Michael a salute before jetting off to his own home.

Michael is so busy pondering the nights events that he forgets about protocol and lands outside his home, not caring about any possible bystanders nearby. Kelly hears him land and quickly opens the garage.

"What are you doing landing out the front?" she yells, but when she sees him covered in blood her tone changes. "My God! What happened?" she asks as she takes off her robe and covers her husband. When he doesn't reply, she asks again, "babe, what happened?"

"She's dead…" Michael mutters to his wife as he trembles in her arms. "Hannah's dead."

"Oh, babe! Come inside," she says as she presses the buzzer, closing their garage door.

Kelly leads him to their bedroom, turns on the shower and gets her husband in. He stands there, still in shock as she gently washes the blood from his body. No words are spoken; she knows he is grieving and allows him that. When the shower is over she guides him to their bed and cuddles up next to him, hoping that tomorrow will be better.

Chapter 25

The Big Entrance

That same night, Constable Sacks and the creature meet beneath a sewer system.

"The two Angels are strong," the creature tells Megan. "They picked apart twenty of my minions in seconds."

"Yes, but we have a full army, Master," Megan replies, "and one of your brothers will join us?"

"Yes, but there is a bigger picture that you don't see."

"I don't get it."

"Of course you don't!" the creature yells at her.

"I also don't get why we have to keep her alive," Constable Sacks says, looking at Hannah who is lying beside the creature, bloodied and broken.

"She is my insurance!" the creature replies.

"What's the plan now?"

"I am one of the Horseman of the Apocalypse," he announces in a tone which would set fear into even the bravest man. Around him, his minions rile around, growling and snarling. "My name is Deprivation, and I will now make my BIG ENTRANCE!"

Deprivation makes his way into one of the tunnels while Constable Sacks remains behind with his minions.

Deprivation emerges from a sewerage outlet next to the city's river. He places his hand into the water and black tar begins to fill the river, killing the fish and any other marine life in the waterway.

"Ha-ha-ha-ha, yes!" Deprivation chuckles to himself, then he goes back into the tunnel and returns to where Constable Sacks is waiting for him.

Seeing that her master has a smile on his face she asks, "Where did you go?"

"Just setting the stage," Deprivation replies.

Hannah murmurs in her sleep as she slowly begins to regain consciousness, which disturbs Deprivation.

"KEEP HER UNCONSCIOUS!" he yells.

"Quick!" Megan shouts to one of the minions near Hannah, but it didn't understand and instead looks puzzled at them both. Megan rushes over to try and knock Hannah out, but she opens her eyes and whispers, "Michael!"

Constable Sacks reaches for her gun and whacks the angel across the head, knocking her unconscious again.

"Hannah!" Michael shouts as he wakes from his sleep. He reaches for his phone and checks the time. It was only two. He stays awake, hoping to hear from Hannah again, but nothing happens. "Was it a dream?" he wonders to himself as he reaches for the water bottle on his bedside table. He lies back down, hoping to fall asleep again.

Meanwhile, back in the sewers, Deprivation growls at Constable Sacks.

"That was close," Megan says as she holsters her gun.

"Nothing close about it!" Deprivation shouts, "SHE SAID HIS NAME!"

"Why is that important?"

"Angels can speak telepathically to one another just by saying the name of the angel they wish to speak with," Deprivation explains.

"So…her saying his name just now…does that mean he heard it?" Megan asks.

"YES!" Deprivation replies. "The element of surprise is gone, but no matter; we will use her as bait! This means we have to do things a little earlier than I expected."

"I'm ready," Constable Sacks replies. "Just say when, Master."

"Not yet. I am waiting for our air soldiers and the news they bring," he says as he looks up through the moonlit grate covering the hole above them.

"The angel is healing rapidly," Megan notes. "Is this going to be a concern later?"

"Angels heal a lot faster than us, but this is not a problem. We just need to snare one of the others then kill them both. The less angels we have to deal with the better!"

Kelly wakes at sunrise to the smell of breakfast. She looks at the other side of the bed to find her husband is already up. She checks her phone for the time and finds it has just ticked over to six.

"What!" Kelly cries. She couldn't believe that she slept in. She jumps out of bed and freshens up, then she walks into the kitchen and asks Michael, "What's going on?"

"Just starting my day. Oh, and good morning, hun!" he says as he rushes over to kiss her. "Your coffee is almost ready," he says as he sips from his own cup. "I wanted yours to be fresh."

"You need to do something with that," Kelly tells Michael, pointing towards the one present left under the Christmas tree.

"Yes, I'll try give it to him today," he sighs.

"No news today?"

"Not yet. I was waiting for you to wake up and for my coffee to prepare me for whatever the news has in store for me today!" he replies, as he sprinkles chocolate powder over her coffee.

"Thanks for the love, babe," Kelly says with a smile.

They make their way to their armchairs in front of the TV. Michael reaches for the remote and looks over at his wife, who gives him a nod as she sips from her cup.

'*...as you can see behind me the river has been contaminated by an un-yet identified substance, and we're already seeing marine life washing up on the banks the whole way through the city,*" a reporter is saying as they flick on to a rolling news channel.

Kelly looks over at her husband in shock. "What now?"

"This has 'biblical' written all over it," Michael replies grimly, then he hears Father Brian's voice in his head, *'Michael!'*

"NO!" Michael says out loud.

'Don't you say 'no' to me!' the priest scolds him. *'Get over here now!'*

"Argh!" Michael groans

"Father Brian?" Kelly asks.

"Yes, he must be watching the same news report as we are."

"Babe, it's on every channel," Kelly tells him. "EVERYONE is watching the same report as we are."

"Well, I better go see what he wants," he says, getting up. Kelly follows him into their bedroom and watches him get dressed.

"Babe, are you ok?" she asks.

"I'm fine!"

"You were distraught last night," Kelly reminds him. "I'm here if you want to talk about it."

"I know, but I'm okay," he says, pulling on a shirt.

"What if I need to talk?"

Michael stops at the bedroom door and looks back at his wife. He can see she needs to get something off her chest. "Are YOU okay, hun?" he asks his wife as he reaches for her hand.

"I don't want you to get hurt," she says quietly "Seeing you covered with all that blood last night made me realise that this is getting dangerous."

"I know, I know. I promise to be careful," Michael says as he wipes away a tear before it has a chance to fall. "I'll be quick, then I'll drop the present off and we can do whatever you want today."

"Okay," she says with a small, forced smile.

"I should be back within the hour."

Michael gives Kelly a kiss on the forehead before he leaves the house.

During the short drive to the church he contemplates everything that has happened up until now. He pulls into the church parking lot and as he hops out of his car he hears an argument inside the church. Father Brian is shouting at someone.

He walks into the church and looks around for Father Brian. He is yelling into his phone, but he gives Michael a hand signal to indicate he will be with him in a minute.

Michael nods to Father Brian, then he blesses himself and walks to the front of the church. He sits down in the front pew by the altar and looks up at the Virgin Mary and the angel murals next to her. One in particular catches his eye. The angel is holding a sword in his hand and his foot is resting on top of a demon's severed head. However, Michael is more intrigued about the object in the angel's other hand which glows slightly as he stares at it.

"Michael?" Father Brian says, breaking his concentration.

"Yes?" Michael says as he looks at the priest.

"Are you okay?" Father Brian asks.

"Yeah, I just got a little distracted!" Michael replies as he shakes his head to clear his vision. "Is that the Archangel Michael?" he asks, pointing at the picture.

"Yes, it is," Father Brian confirms.

"Is it meant to symbolise something?"

"It doesn't depict anything in particular other than the Angel Michael slaying a demon—"

"What's that in his hand?"

"His sword, which makes Michael that much mightier—"

"No! *That*!" Michael says, pointing towards the other object.

"A set of scales," Father Brian explains. "He is slaying one of the horsemen of the Apocalypse, known as Famine. In the Bible, it describes that Famine comes once the Horseman of War has arrived. Which brings me to why I asked you here today. Now—"

"Father?" Michael interrupts him yet again, "Is it possible that the Horseman Famine is already here on Earth?"

"Why you ask?"

"Just a hunch."

Father Brian says firmly, "I'm going to need more than a hunch to convince me that the Apocalypse has arrived."

"Okay, okay," Michael says,, "What if I told you that I see or dream things?"

"Like premonitions?"

"Kind of. Before the attack on the Pope, I dreamt of a Bloodied Horse"

"Bloodied, you say?" Father Brian interjects.

"Yes, why? Is that important?"

"Well, that would make it a redhorse, wouldn't you say?"

"Yes, but what does that mean?" Michael asks.

"In Revelations 6:4 it says: '...and there went out another horse that was RED, and power was given to him that sat thereon to take peace from the Earth.'"

"WHAT!" Michael cries, shocked

"This Horseman is called WAR!" Father Brian whispers as his eyes well up. "The Apocalypse is upon us!"

"What did you say about the second Horseman, Father?" Michael asks.

"Famine," the priest whispers.

"Yes, and that he followed after War!" Michael says. "I think there are two Horsemen on Earth!"

Father Brian falls to his knees in shock. "That explains it!"

"Explains what, Father?"

"The OMEN!"

"What omen?"

"That's why I was on the phone to the Vatican. They also saw the omen and demanded that I get you to do something about it!"

"Father, what omen?" Michael grabs hold of the priest, helps him to his feet and sits him down on the pew in front of him.

"The omen on the news this morning," he says, looking at Michael. "Revelation 8:8-9: 'All ablaze was thrown into the sea. A third of the sea turned into blood, a third of the living creatures in the sea died'. As I said, the Apocalypse is upon us! You and the other Angels are not enough for this."

He stands up and begins to walk towards the presbytery.

"Where are you going, Father?"

"To let the Vatican know and to say goodbye to my loved ones. More importantly, to pray," he says as he walks away, his body slumped in defeat.

Michael rushes out of the church and speeds back to his home. "Come on, come on!" he says as he presses his garage remote, frantically trying to get it to open quickly. He parks his car and rushes inside the house crying loudly, "KEL! KEL!"

"What, what?" she answers as she rushes to him in the lounge.

"You need to go, with the kids!"

"WHAT! WHERE? WHAT'S GOING ON?"

"Both Father Brian and I think that the Apocalypse is coming!"

"The Apocalypse? Isn't that like the end of the world stuff?" Kelly asks.

"YES!" Michael answers.

"Well, then there is nowhere we can hide. Anyway, what makes you so sure it's coming?"

"We think two Horsemen of the Apocalypse are on Earth!" Michael replies. "Remember the red horse cloud above the Vatican when the Pope died?"

"Yes," she replies.

"The name of the Horseman that rides a red Horse, is the Horseman of WAR!" Michael says.

"The Declaration of War!" Kelly whispers under her breath

"I'm sorry what?" Michael replies.

"The message at the Pope's house, remember? 'We have killed your leader! You are now leaderless'. That was basically a Declaration of War, He declared himself from the start, we just didn't understand it! But that's only one Horseman and it's in ROME!"

"Well, Father said the Bible described Famine as a Horseman that follows when War has arrived!"

"Yes, but the Bible is thousands of years of scriptures. What's the chance of it actually coming to pass?"

"I don't know, but I'm not taking any chances," Michael replies.

Michael doesn't explain why he strongly believes that the other Horseman, Famine, has arrived as well. He contemplates the image of the Archangel Michael and the glowing scales he saw earlier, which symbolises the horseman Famine.

"Michael? Michael? Helloooo?" Kelly says loudly, waving her hand before his eyes.

"Yes, sorry," Michael apologises.

"Where'd you go?"

"Nowhere. I just have a lot to think about."

"Are you going to tell Quinn? I think you should!"

"Yeah, maybe later," Michael says.

"Well, don't leave it too late. 'Cos you still have to visit your brother and give him that present," she said as she walks off to their bedroom to sort out their laundry.

"Good Lord! I'll do it now," Michael says.

"You may as well get some lunch while you're out," Kelly adds.

"Yes, dear!" he replies in a snide manner.

He opens the garage and hops into his car, then he closes his eyes and calls, "Quinn? Are you there?"

After a long, worrying silence Quinn finally responds, *'Yeah?'*

"Are you okay?" Michael asks

'I'm fine,' Quinn deflects, the roughness in his voice barely concealing the emotion.

"I need to see you. Can we meet?"

'Yeah, sure,' Quinn replies, *'I'm on Queens Street.'*

"What number?" Michael asks, but he's met by silence. "Quinn, what number?" he asks again, worried. "QUINN! Don't do anything silly!" Michael shouts, then he speeds out of his garage and rushes off to his street.

"Quinn, I'm here! Where are you?" he asks in a stern manner while driving his car slowly down Queens Street, hoping to find him. Huge feathers begin to fall from the sky.

"QUINN!" Michael shouts as he hops out of his car and looks up. The feathers are falling from the top of a five-storey apartment building. Michael runs towards the side of the building complex next to the bins. He looks around for bystanders and, seeing none, flies upwards.

"Please be okay, please be okay!" Michael whispers to himself, then when he reaches the top he sees Quinn walking around aimlessly ripping away the feathers from his wings.

"Quinn, what are you doing?" Michael asks, trying to read the situation..

"They grow back almost instantly," Quinn tells him.

"What?" Michael replies.

"The feathers, they grow back instantly. Watch!"

Quinn rips away one feather and another feather immediately appears in its place.

Michael sees Quinn's phone lying on the ground. He picks it up and sees a picture of Hannah.

"We swapped numbers," Quinn tells Michael sadly. "I liked her, and I think she liked me."

He begins to cry. Michael doesn't know what to say, so instead he hugs Quinn, who weeps into his chest.

"I didn't know!" Michael says as a tear falls from his eye and they both grieve for their fallen comrade.

"You said you wanted to talk?" Quinn says as he uses his shirt to wipe his tears away

"Uh, it can wait."

"You sure? It sounded urgent."

"Yeah, I'm sure. Right now I want to spend some time with a friend," Michael says with a smile. They both sit on some folding chairs on the roof, then Quinn says, "I've got a question."

"Okay, shoot," Michael says

"If God made us angels, then why did he let her die?"

"That's a good question, Quinn," Michael replies, "I'm not going to attempt to be God and guess why He does the things He does,"

"That's the right answer," Quinn says in response. "I don't need a preachers answer. You know, that 'God moves in mysterious ways' CRAP! An honest answer!"

"You okay?" Michael says as he gives Quinn a pat on the shoulder. He stands as if to leave, but he needs to be sure Quinn is okay first.

Quinn is silent, then he looks up at Michael and says, "I don't think I want to fight for Him anymore."

"Then don't!" Michael says. "Fight for me!"

"That I can do," Quinn agrees with a smile.

"Stay in touch and stay safe."

"Why do you keep saying that?"

"'Cos, I want you to be safe!" Michael says as he smiles back at him, then he jumps off the roof and uses his wings to float down to the ground. Michael draws in a big breath and closes his eyes, troubled by Quinn's emotional state. He lets go of the breath and walks to his car, then as he gets in he then notices his brother's present.

"Damn it!" he mutters as he drives off. After twenty minutes he arrives at his brother's house, but his car is not in the driveway.

"Great! Already on the drink!" Michael says as he heads in the direction of a nearby bar. As he approaches, he spots his brother's car in the parking lot. "Like clockwork!" he says as he parks his own car and grabs his brother's present.

When Michael walks into the bar already he sees three lonely souls. Two drunk males are placing bets on the local races while the other is sitting in the corner of the bar staring into his drink.

"Bingo!" Michael said as he walks over to Ambrose.

"What do you want?" Ambrose asks as Michael gets closer. Michael reaches for a chair to sit down, but his brother says, "That seat is taken."

"Hmm, okay," Michael replies.

"Well? What do you want?" Ambrose demands, glaring at his brother with hatred.

"I wanted to give you this," Michael said as he offers him the wrapped Christmas present.

"I don't want it!"

Ignoring him, Michael places it on the table.

"I SAID I DON'T WANT IT!" Ambrose yells, swiping the present off the table.

It was a coffee mug which smashed against the wall.

"Your nephews made that for you!" Michael says as he turns away. Ambrose felt stupid as he calmed down. Michael starts to walk away, but then he stops and walked back with anger on his face. "Why do you hate me so much?"

"COS ITS ALWAYS ABOUT YOU!" Ambrose shouts as he stands up to be at eye level with his brother. "You were always the favourite child who could do no wrong in Mum and Dad's eyes!"

"That's not true!" Michael retorts.

"Yes, it is! They put you high upon a pedestal and we got treated like shit for it! All because we couldn't reach the same heights that you did," he says with a touch of sorrow.

"As each of our brothers died, they got more and more relentless with us. Picking away at our confidence and telling us that we would never amount to half the things you did!"

Michael has never seen this side of his brother before,.

"And where were you, when all of this was happening?" Ambrose asks as anger returns to his voice.

"I created a family, Ambrose," Michael replies. "You can't blame me for that!"

"Oh, I can, and I will! We wanted our big brother to come and save us, but he didn't," Ambrose's voice cracks with barely concealed emotion.

Michael can tell his brother needed to get this off his chest. "Ambrose, I'm sorry!" he says, trying to hold back his own tears. "I didn't know!"

"Yeah, well you're no brother to me if you couldn't see that I was suffering!"

"I suffered too, Ambrose."

"Bullshit!"

"Yes, I did!" Michael yells, and Ambrose listens for the first time. "Every time you or any of our brothers got hurt, got bullied or damaged something in the house, who do you think got disciplined? Remember when you climbed onto the roof and fell?"

"Yeah, why?" Ambrose asks.

"Mum took you to get stitches while I stayed home and got the cord from Dad because I was the eldest and I should have known better," Michael says, getting upset as he recalls this injustice.

"You couldn't walk for a week," Ambrose murmurs. He has calmed down and feels some sympathy for Michael, but he doesn't show it to his brother. He has too much pride for that.

There is a silence between them that neither knows how to break, so Michael slowly turns and walks away. He stops at the entrance of the bar and asks, "Do you know the difference between being strong and having strength?"

Ambrose doesn't answer.

"Being strong is a physical ability," Michael continues. "Me and you, we have a strength quality."

"Which means what?" Ambrose asks.

"We're resilient. No matter what life throws at us, we can take it, and we're stronger for the experience," Michael says, before smiling at his brother and walking out.

Ambrose contemplates his brother's words, then he looks over at the present he smashed. He picks it up, places it on the table and unwraps it. The mug is broken, but there's another item inside. He picks up the black shirt, and holding it up sees that it is printed with the message: 'Our uncle is a superhero'.

"Those ratbags!" he whispers under his breath. He takes off his old shirt and puts on the new one.

"Nice fit!" the bartender compliments Ambrose.

"Thanks. My nephews made it!" he said with a smile.

"Lucky guy! It looks good on you, Bro!"

"Hey, do you have any super glue?" Ambrose asks.

"I think so. Let me check."

"Thanks!" Ambrose says.

"Here you go!" the bartender says as he tosses him the tube. Ambrose catches it and gets to work fixing the broken mug.

While Michael is driving back home he sees police cars speed by in the opposite direction.

"Wonder what's going on?" he mutters as he turns on his car radio.

'...*fire crews are attending as we report live from the boat ramp. In case you're just joining us, the river itself has mysteriously caught alight...*'

Michael shakes his head in disbelief.

'*Everyone is urged to stay indoors and stay clear of the vicinity.*'

Michael calls his wife.

"Hey Babe!"

"Kel! Turn on the news!" Michael shouts.

"Why?"

"Please just do it and put me on speaker!"

Kelly rushes to find the remote on the coffee table. She turns on the TV and sees a news report showing the river on fire. Black smoke is polluting the sky and people are running for safety from nearby buildings.

We are unsure how the Swan River has caught fire, but it's safe to say that no one should be in the vicinity. We just pray that everyone has been safely evacuated!"

"My God!" Kelly says out loud, "Its begun!"

Hearing his wife's nervousness, Michael asks, "Is it bad?"

Kelly doesn't respond

"You there?"

"Sorry, yes. Michael you should see this. It's getting dark; there's fire everywhere. It's like the city is going to go up in flames! Where are you now?"

"On my way home. I should be there in five or ten minutes."

"Maybe you should turn around?" Kelly suggests.

"What! No! Fire and emergency should take care of it!"

"Not this type of fire," she responds, still mesmerised by what she's seeing on the screen.

"Just hold on, I'm just another street away," Michael replies before he ends the call and accelerates. "QUINN!"

'Yeah?

"Are you watching the news?"

'No, I'm still up on the roof!'

"Get to a TV," Michael insists. "Something is happening on the river that needs our attention!"

'Okay, I'm going down to my apartment now', Quinn says as he races to the door that leads to the stairwell. He races down a few flights of stairs to his floor, then he bursts into his apartment and turns the TV on. His jaw drops when he sees the entire river ablaze. *Michael, is this that BIG something that's coming for us?'*

"I don't know," Michael replies with uncertainty and sorrow. "I don't know."

Michael arrives home and races into the lounge to find Kelly glued to the TV. "Babe, it's getting worse! The blaze is getting closer to a few smaller buildings on the foreshore. Look!"

As she points at the screen, creatures are seen crawling out of the sewers near the foreshore. They burst into one of the smaller buildings, possibly looking for people who have yet to evacuate.

"What the hell are those?" Kelly gasps in horror, then Quinn asks, *Michael, are you seeing this?*

"Yes, there're more of them," Michael says with shock.

'An army of them.'

Deprivation exits the tunnels holding Hannah who is still unconscious. The helicopters surrounding the area shine their spotlights on them both. Deprivation holds Hannah into the air by her neck, choking her as he raises her. He is taunting the other angels by showing even they aren't strong enough to stop him.

Chapter 26

Code of the Hero

Michael stares in horror at this new foe who is torturing Hannah. He is dressed in black with a tattered cloak and a war helmet, a vertical grill shields his face.

'Quinn?' Michael calls.

No answer.

"QUINN!" Michael shouts, but there is still no answer.

"What's the matter?" Kelly asks.

"I think Quinn is going to do something stupid!" Michael replies as he races to get his suit.

"And where are you going?" Kel calls after him, scared and nervous.

"I have to go!" Michael says as he suits up. "Quinn is going to get himself killed!"

"THAT IS AN ARMY!" Kelly yells out loud, startling the kids who are now in the lounge watching the news.

"Dad? Mum?" Emma calls as she sits with her brothers. "What's going on?"

Kelly and Michael return to the lounge. Seeing that her father is wearing his angel suit, Emma asks with concern, "Where are you going?"

"There!" Michael says, nodding towards the TV with his head.

"You can't!" Emma cries in alarm. "There are way too many of them!"

"Hun, who else is going to stop them?"

Emma doesn't answer. Instead she stares at the screen..

"Remember what you told me before?" Michael asks. "A hero has an obligation to protect people, whether he has a family or not."

"Yeah, but that was before I knew the Angel was you!" she protests.

"I promise to come right back," he tells his family, "and I keep my promises."

"You better come back; I swear to GOD!" Kelly threatens her husband.

"I will," he says as he turns to leave through the front door, then as a further safety measure he silently calls out, *'Father Brian? Can you hear me?'*

"Yes, Michael," he answers, surprised that Michael was able to contact him without prayer.

'I was hoping you could do me a favour.'

"Anything. What is it?"

'Could you pray for me? I would very much like to make it back to my family!'

"That I can do!" the priest responds, then he kneels and bows his head while Michael does the same thing on his front lawn.

'Lord, I pray for you to watch over your angels. Michael faithfully places his life in your hands as he fights to protect us all. He asks that you guide him to safety and back into his family's loving arms. Amen!'"

"Amen!" Michael repeats as he blesses himself, then he rises and prepares to face the new evil that has surfaced. He looks towards the city in the distance and can see half the night sky is lit up by the blaze. He bends his knees until they are almost touching the ground, then raises his hands and wings. Both curl, as if to grip a piece of the air, then he pulls downwards propelling himself high up into the air, even higher than usual. Once he is above the clouds he turns to see his destination and surges towards the city with a sense of urgency.

'Give 'em Hell!' Father Brian whispers.

Michael smirks and flies faster than he ever has before.

The possessed humans run rampant throughout the city, damaging anything and everything in their path. They find and drag out three people from a convenience store that failed to evacuate.

"Please don't!" the store owner cries out.

"Please let us go!" a woman cries with tears streaming down her face. Her husband crawls in front, trying to shield her.

The three creatures fight over their food. They snap at each other and the foam from their mouths sprays everywhere as they fight. The humans try to crawl away unseen, but they are dragged back by their feet. They glance at each other, then as one of the rabid humans' lunges at them, they close their eyes and scream.

There is a sudden loud thump followed by a wet slap.

The woman opens her eyes to see her husband shielding her. Wondering what had happened, they turn and see the creatures lying dead on the ground, then they look up and see Quinn. The angel has his back turned towards them and is keeping a watchful eye out for more danger.

"Get to safety!" he tells them, clenching his teeth.

"Thank you!" the woman says.

"Thank you, thank you!" the husband and store owner add as they get up and run as fast as they can.

"Look! It's one of the angels!" a bystander cries out, then a crowd of regular people came racing out from the other buildings.

"WHAT!?" Quinn cries, shocked. "Why haven't you all evacuated?"

"Everything happened so fast," one of the shop attendants explains. "It was just a fire at first, but then these creatures made it impossible to evacuate. There was no time!"

"Get behind me everyone!" he shouts, annoyed that they were preventing him from his mission to save Hannah. "There are police and emergency services down the street. When I say go, you all run towards them as fast as you can! GOT IT?"

"YES!" they all confirm.

"Get ready!" he says as he sees five creatures making their way towards them, then a further six more creatures arrive and they all rush towards him. When they are only a few metres away, Quinn rushed towards them while crying to the others, "RUNNNN!"

His wings twirl and cut down the first two creatures with ease, then he grabs hold of two others with his hands. They jump on Quinn and start snapping their jaws at him. This distraction enables the people to escape and made it to the end of the street where they are greeted by the police and emergency personnel. Some of the evacuees are crying from sheer exhaustion while others tremble at finally making it out of harm's way.

"Someone has to help him!" one of the lady bystanders tells a police officer. "He's going to die!"

"Who?" the constable asks.

"The angel that saved us!" she cries hysterically. "He needs help, please!"

"Ma'am, we can't! It's too dangerous, even for us!" he replies with sorrow. Everyone who was saved stand behind the police barrier and watch Quinn from afar, weeping for their saviour and praying that he survives.

Quinn is momentarily overcome by his attackers, but then he thinks about Hannah and how helpless she looked on the news with the bigger creature holding her as hostage.

"Aargh!" he screams in frustration, then he smashes two of the creatures together, killing them instantly. He then grabs the creature on his back, flings it over his head and smashes it down in front of him. Another creature took a backward step, afraid.

"Get out of my face!" Quinn roars, then using his wings he slaps it away, crushing it against a building.

Quinn breathes heavily. Bloodied, he walks towards the inner city where Hannah is being held by the large creature. Deprivation is sitting down on a throne made of rubble with the unconscious Hannah lying beside him.

"Ah, finally an angel!" Deprivation says as he sees Quinn walking towards him, giving him a death stare. "And where's the big guy?"

"It's not him you have to worry about!" Quinn says menacingly to Deprivation. "Give her back to me or you die!

"Ah, you have feelings for this one," Deprivation replies. "Well, that makes her more valuable!"

"You piece of shit!" Quinn shouts as he flies towards him.

Deprivation reaches down and places his plague-ridden hands on Hannah's throat.

"No please!" Quinn stops and raises his hands to stop Deprivation of harming her

"Down on your knees!" Deprivation commands and Quinn drops instantly.

A news helicopter flies above capturing the event while the whole world anxiously watches on, fearing they are about to see another angel die.

Deprivation walks towards Quinn dragging a spear behind him.

"Do you know the only thing that can kill an angel?"
"What?"

"A spear made from HELL! Mixed with a special ingredient, of course," Deprivation says, trying to scare Quinn. "The other angels died instantly when I skewered them!"

"Just do it; don't bore me!" Quinn retorts, showing Deprivation that he doesn't fear death.

"Alright then," Deprivation says as he grips the spear with both hands and raises it high into the air, ready to plunge it into Quinn.

"No! Please!" all the bystanders behind the police barrier yell out.

Quinn stares into Deprivations eyes, not showing him any emotion other than anger. He doesn't want his enemy to see how afraid he really is.

The fire on the river suddenly goes out, momentarily distracting Deprivation. Quinn acts quickly and punches him, sending him flying and crashing into a nearby building.

"Hannah!" Quinn cries as he rushes over to her. "Hannah!"

He tries to wake her, and she moves slightly, showing some sign of life.

Michael lands beside Quinn with a loud thump. "Get her out of here!" he cries as he looks around for danger.

"That's easier said than done," Quinn replies as he cradles Hannah in his arms and looks at the evil army that has surrounded them.

"I'll give you cover," Michael says as he prepares to fight. "Just get her far from here!"

"What about you?"

"I'll be fine!" Michael replies. "Now go!"

"Thank you!" Quinn said, looking at Michael with admiration, then he leaps into the air and his wings take him high above where the creatures can't go.

Michael stands watching him, unaware that Constable Sacks is lurking in the shadows as he watches the army making their way towards him.

"Argh!" Megan cries as she lunges forward and swipes at him with the spear.

Michael is caught off guard; he raises his hands in defence and his left hand is sliced by the spear.

"Aargh!" he yells in agony. He knows that the spear is deadly to angels, so he knocks it out of Megan's grasp with his right hand. He then grips her throat tightly in anger and as he does this her eyes light up yellow and glow intensely.

"No, No, No!" she cries hysterically. "It's me, it's me! The demon's gone! He's gone!"

A four-storey building quaked. Michael looks towards it and sees Deprivation walking out from the rubble and dusting himself off.

Upon seeing Michael, Deprivation smiles and whistles a high-pitched and very long whistle. Michael lets go of Constable Sacks as he hears more growls coming from above. The pair stand there watching the skies, then they hear swooping.

"Get behind me!" Michael orders Megan. "When the time is right, you run! Don't wait. Just run!"

"Got it!"

Two demon-like creatures swoop out from the thick black smoke lingering from the blaze.

"CRAP!" Michael shouts as he can do nothing except hold his ground. He raises his hands and wings to hold off the demon attack. While wrestling with the two demons, Michael looks over to Constable Sacks, his muscles trembling as he holds them off.

"Go, now!" he cries.

Megan runs as fast as she can, but the demons don't follow, remaining focussed on Michael.

Deprivation sees Constable Sacks escaping and realises that the demon within her must have been extinguished by Michael. Megan is too valuable to let live; she knows too much. Deprivation shoves the broken building which topples in her direction.

Megan screams.

"No!" Michael shouts, then he frees himself from the clutches of the two demons and flies towards Megan who curls up in a brace position. "Hold on!"

Michael can't swoop in and pick her up without the building hitting them both, so he catches the building instead and spreads his wings out helping to balance it. His face is anguished and he trembles from the weight as he drops to one knee.

"Please run!" he tells Megan.

"Thank you!" she says, then as she sprints for safety she calls out, "They know where you live!"

"How touching!" Deprivation says as four-winged demons land beside him. "You two," he pointed at a pair, "go and find the other two angels. The rest come with me."

Michael is trying to lift the building off his wings without getting crushed in the process, but he can't.

"What's the matter?" Deprivation taunts. "Bit off more than you can chew?"

Sensing danger, Michael tries to get to his feet and deadlifts the entire building.

When Deprivation gives the two demons a nod, they jump onto the building, adding more weight for Michael to carry. He falls back to one knee, huffing and puffing as he struggles with the extra burden. The weight proves too much. Michael is flattened into the ground and the building breaks in two.

Deprivation laughs, enjoying the moment.

The two demons dig into the rubble and pull Michael out by his wings. He is unconscious and his suit is torn to shreds. Deprivation points towards the helicopter circling above, then he points towards Michael and laughs.

Chapter 27

The Wrath of Quinn

Hannah stirs and slowly begins to wake in Quinn's arms. She looks up at him and sees that he looks nervous, the wind is rushing past them as he flies faster than ever before.

"What's happening?" Hannah asks softly.

"Hannah! You're okay!" Quinn exclaims. "Just take it easy."

Hannah can hear the tension in his voice. She looks behind them and sees two winged demons in pursuit.

"Get back here, Angel!" one shouts, trying to get closer, but Quinn is too fast.

"What are those things?" Hannah asks, disturbed.

"I'll explain later; right now, I need to think!" He finds a suitable spot below and says, "Okay, I'm going to put you down on that roof top—"

"Quinn—"

He interrupts her before she has a chance to speak. "It's going to be okay." He then lands and places Hannah gently on the roof top before turning to face the approaching demons. Quinn grabs hold of one, but the other demon slips past him, its wings grazing him on the leg.

"Shit!" Quinn says as it rushes towards Hannah.

Quinn managed to grip the demon, but only partially. The demon is snapping and clawing at Hannah who tries to use her wings to protect herself, but her missing wing has not fully grown back yet; it's only half a wing with a pointy nub.

"Argh!" Quinn grunts as he struggles to hold a demon in each hand. Hannah tries to help Quinn by crawling away, but the pain in her leg is almost unbearable.

"Ah, come on!" Hannah urges herself. She manages to reach the edge and looks down.

"Shit, too far to drop!" she says, so she rests her back against the wall, hoping she had helped Quinn enough.

Quinn is still struggling against the two demons. One claws at Quinn, leaving his arm bloodied. The other demon drags them both towards Hannah, as it hasn't yet given up trying to reach her. When it starts to snap at her feet she curls up into a foetal position and screams.

"Hannah!" Quinn cries as he feels himself being dragged along by the Demon who is straining to reach Hannah. "Please God, no!" he prays, closing his eyes.

"There is no God, Angel!" the Demon taunts Quinn as he stops struggling, for he wants to watch his comrade rip Hannah apart. He smiles as the other demon edges closer and closer.

"Quinn!" Hannah screams

"Hannah!"

Quinn contemplates sacrificing himself by letting go of his demon to grab a hold of the one going for Hannah.

Suddenly, too fast to see it happen, something swoops down from the sky.

Quinn sees that the demon in his hand is gone. "WHAT?" he cries, shocked that something or someone had helped him.

"Quinn!" Hannah cries out.

"Hannah!" Quinn grabs hold of the wing of the remaining demon, he lifts it up and slams it back down again away from Hannah. She looks up and sees Quinn standing in front of her, ready to defend her. As they trade blows the winged demon knows he is no match for Quinn; Hannah is his only weakness, so he has to find a way to reach her.

"You're pissing me off, Angel!" the demon shouts angrily.

"Good!" Quinn smiles, gaining confidence by the minute.

The demon snarls, then he flies head on at Quinn.

Quinn tries to finish the demon in one blow, but it dodges him and takes him down with a manoeuvre with his legs.

As Quinn crashes to the ground, the demon is quick to reach Hannah and takes her as hostage.

"Quinn! Help!" Hannah cries.

"NO!" Quinn replies, then he warns the demon, "If you hurt her…!"

"What?" the demon threatens. "You have nothing to bargain; nothing to threaten me with. I hold all the cards! You Angels are all brawn and no brains!"

The demon holds its claws up to Hannah's throat.

"Please don't!" Quinn pleads.

The demon smiles at Quinn, then it digs its claw into Hannah, who screams

"Hannah!" Quinn cries out as he takes a few steps towards them, but the demon raises its other hand, halting him.

"BACK!" the Demon commands.

Quinn screws up his face as he reluctantly retreats, then he threatens, "I swear to God! If you hurt her..!"

The demon and Quinn lock eyes. No words are spoken as they study one another carefully.

"HAH!" the demon said as it raises its hand, ready to plunge its claws into Hannah. Quinn runs as fast as he can trying to stop it, but he knows he would be unable to reach her in time.

Hannah acts quickly. Extending her wings, she stabs the demon with her half wing which plunges deep into its chest, wounding it.

Seizing his opportunity Quinn flies towards the demon and grabs hold of it.

"GOTCHA!" Quinn says, then he flies up into the air and tries to suffocate the demon with his wings. Quinn only sees RED as he squeezes the demon tight like a boa constrictor, crushing every bone in its body.

"I told you not to touch her." Quinn whispers to the demon before he lets it drop to the ground with a wet sound

Hannah watches as Quinn descends to her. As she sits upright against the rooftop wall she asks, "Was that sound the demon?"

"Yep!" Quinn replies.

"A little much, don't you think?"

"Well, I told him not to touch my…uh… you," Quinn stumbles.

"Just get over here!" she says with a laugh.

"Yes, Ma'am!" Quinn replies as he sits beside her.

"Quinn, how can I…?"

"What?"

"Men, I swear!" Hannah replies as she turns towards him, grabs his tattered shirt and pulls him towards her so they could FINALLY share a much-needed kiss.

Chapter 28

Brothers in Arms

Deprivation finds his spear lying on the ground and picks it up. The pair of winged demons drag Michael's body up onto a pile of rubble which leads towards the makeshift throne.

"Is he dead?" one of the demons asks Deprivation.

"Let's find out," he replies, then he lifted his spear high into the air and plunges it into Michael's left shoulder, who cries out in agony.

"There we are! He lives!" Deprivation laughs, then he cruelly wriggles the spear from left to right whilst it is still in Michael's shoulder.

"Aargh!" Michael screams, then he coughs up blood as Deprivation withdraws the spear.

"Place him on the throne!" Deprivation commands his minions.

Michael moans as the pair of demons drag him towards the throne, lift him up and dump him upon it. His wings droop down over his body to shield him.

"No!" Deprivation yells. "Hold his wings! They will protect him!"

The demons grabbed hold of each wing and hold them apart. Deprivation smiles as he adjusts his spear and aims it at Michael's head. Looking up, he see's the helicopter which is no doubt broadcasting the event. Again the demon smiles to himself, pleased to be showing the world that their precious angels just weren't enough.

"Babe, NO!" Kelly cries at the TV, she covers her mouth sobbingly. "GET UP!" she continued to scream.

Deprivation looks back at Michael, he adjusts his gaze and points the spear at Michael's head.A cruel grin spread across his face, he hurls the spear which spirals swiftly towards him.

A black spiral of death cutting through the smoke-filled sky. Time seamed fractured. Every heartbeat slowed. The world held its breath as the spear streaked towards Michael's head.

'SWOOP!'

A gust of wind swiftly makes the spear disappear before Deprivation's eyes. He snarls as he looks around. He can hear the flap of wings high above, circling him, then a whistling sound. Deprivation dives out of the way as his own spear was thrown back at him.

'SWOOP!'

One of the demons that is holding Michael hostage disappears, then black blood begins to trickle down like rain before the torso of the dead demon falls from the sky.

'THUD!'

Someone lands in front of them, but it is not an angel, for its wings are like those of a bat.

Deprivation growls and snarls at the intruder who points towards Michael and says, "LET MY BROTHER GO!"

"Ambrose!" Michael croaks as he recognises his voice.

Deprivation tells Ambrose, "The Boss won't be happy with this!"

"This wasn't a part of the deal!" he shouts.

"The deal was to kill angels!" Deprivation reminds him. "Your brother is an angel! What part of the deal is unclear?"

"He failed to mention my brother was an angel!"

"He will take your soul for this, Ambrose!" Deprivation yells.

"He already has it!" Ambrose shouts in reply.

"Ambrose, NO!" Michael cried.

"I just need to die for him to claim it," Ambrose says as he looks over at his battered brother, "which is not happening anytime soon!"

"I can make that happen!" Deprivation says as he tugs his spear out of the ground.

Michael yanks his wing free from the demon's clutches and gives it a kick. He then flies towards Ambrose, and they stand back-to-back, each facing a foe.

Chapter 29

Set Aside the Pride

Two brothers are now all that stands in the way of the world's destruction by the forces of darkness.

"You know, you have a lot to explain," Michael says to Ambrose.

"I could say the same about you!"

"How about we kill them first, talk later?"

"Agreed!" Ambrose replies.

"Do you want to swap?" Michael asks.

"No! I want the Horseman!" Ambrose says. "I have a bone to pick with him!"

"Come on, then!" Deprivation taunts.

Ambrose yells in anger as he flies towards Deprivation, then they fall into a knot of limbs on the ground in a battle of sheer strength.

"Ambrose!" Michael cries out, but the other demon says, "Worry about yourself, Angel!"

It flies swiftly towards Michael, landing a blow on his face which brings him to his knees.

"Is that all?" Michael asks as he turns his head back towards the demon and gets to his feet.

"WHAT?" the demon cries, taking a backward step. Afraid.

The fight between Deprivation and Ambrose is one-sided. Ambrose falls to one knee, then with a grimace he asks, "Why did you choose me?"

"I didn't!"

"What?" Ambrose replies, stunned, "I know a Horseman did this to me!"

"There are four of us, boy! I wouldn't have recruited you! You're too weak!" Deprivation taunts him.

"Tell me who?" Ambrose pleads, but Deprivation laughs and replies, "NO!"

Ambrose screams as he rises to his feet, almost overpowering Deprivation. He kicks the Horseman repeatedly in the ribs, but it has no affect, and Ambrose has tired himself out. Deprivation just smiles at him, then he grabs hold of Ambrose's throat and asks, "Is that all you have? I told you that I don't recruit weaklings! One of my brothers must have been desperate to choose you!"

Ambrose punches Deprivation in the ribs again and again, then to his jaw.

"You do have a lot of fight, I'll give you that!" the Horseman says as he endures Ambrose's attacks, "but it's time to say goodbye!"

Deprivation grabs hold of his spear.

"Ambrose! No!" Michael cries, then he catches his demon with his hands and flings it at Deprivation.

"ARGH!"

Deprivation topples over as the demon collides with him, then Michael tells his brother, "Okay, I've got the Horseman now!"

"Shut up! I still have him!" Ambrose replies. Then, blinded by rage, he charges at the Horseman.

"AMBROSE!" Michael cries as he chases after his brother, unaware that the other demon is closing in on him. It crashes into Michael and clings to his injured left arm.

Michael screams out in pain.

"I told you to worry about yourself, Angel!" the demon says as it jams a claw into Michael's open wound.

"AHHHHHHH!"

"You might have had me if it weren't for this wound, ha-ha-ha! It slows you down!

"It was all part of the plan!" Michael whispers as he turns his gaze towards the demon.

"WHAT!?" it cries in horror.

Michael grabs the demon by its throat with his right hand. "I've wasted too much time with you. I just needed to get you closer to do this!"

He tightened his grip on the demon's throat and popped its head off its shoulders.

"No one tells me what to do!" Michael says as he tosses the dead demon aside, then he mutters, "Except maybe my wife."

He tries to find Ambrose and the Horseman, but he can't see or hear them.

"AMBROSE!" Michael yells out as he leaps down from the mountain of rubble to the ground. "Ambrose! Can you hear me?"

Michael tries to talk with him through prayer, but there is no reply.

"Ambrose, if you can hear me, say something, anything!"

"Argh, uh!" Ambrose responds.

"AMBROSE!" Michael cries out for his brother. "Where are you?"

Again no response

"AMBROSE!" Michael bellows.

The news helicopter hovering above Michael points the camera at Ambrose and the Horseman who appear on the big screen in the city square. Michael sees Deprivation is choking Ambrose. His brother doesn't seem to have much life left as his legs have stopped kicking. Michael spots the statue of a swan behind Deprivation, which betrays their location. Michael flies towards them and smashes into Deprivation, toppling him into a building.

"Ambrose?" Michael cries out as he gently taps his brother's face. "Ambrose! Are you okay?"

Ambrose struggles to breathe as he clutches his neck. "You found me!"

"If it wasn't for the news helicopter I may not have!" Michael explains.

"Is that so?" Deprivation's voice says from the battered building. He stays in the darkness so the brothers can't see him, but they see a huge block of rubble being flung towards the helicopter. It smashes one of the rotor blades and the aircraft spirals as it struggles to stay in the air.

Everyone inside the helicopter screams in terror. The camera falls to the floor leaving all the viewers at home wondering what's happening.

"NO!" Michael cries out

"GO!" Ambrose tells him.

Michael hesitates, not wanting to leave his brother vulnerable whilst Deprivation is still out there, but Ambrose repeats, "GO! I'll be fine!"

"Don't do anything stupid!" Michael warns him.

"Couldn't if I wanted to!"

Michael flies off to help the people in the helicopter.

"Please help us!" the news reporter cries out hysterically as she reaches out her hand.

"Hold on!" Michael shouts. He reaches for one of the helicopter's landing skids to stabilise it, but before he can do so he is attacked and taken away by Deprivation.

"NOOOOOOO!" the news reporter cries out.

"YES!" Deprivation cries as he begins to lay into Michael, then they land on the ground and begin fighting in earnest.

The helicopter spirals and descends towards the ground; everyone inside screams and holds on tight, bracing for impact.

THUD!

The helicopter is suddenly stable. The passengers look at one another wondering what has happened.

"Is everyone alright?" a pained voice asks.

"YES, we're okay!" they all said in unison.

"Quick, hop out" Ambrose tells them as he tries to place the helicopter down gently, but with his injuries it proves too much for him and it crashes to the ground, destroying both landing skids.

"Okay, get to safety," Ambrose replies, pointing towards a police barrier at the end of the street.

"Can I say something?" the news reporter asks.

"As long as you make it quick!"

"I think you two need to put your ego's aside and work together. You can end this right now if you do!"

Ambrose turns his back on her, not wanting to admit that he needs help.

"Anyway, just putting it out there!"

"What's your name?" Ambrose asked.

"Natalie."

"Thank you, Natalie," Ambrose smiles at her and she smiles back before running to join her work colleagues behind the police barrier.

"Ugh, teamwork!" Ambrose grumbles to himself. "The last thing I want is to be helped by him! Where is Michael, anyway?"

Ambrose sees his brother and the Horseman trading blows in the distance. Extending his demon wings he propels himself in their direction and smashes into Deprivation's shoulder, sending him flying into the air. Ambrose then reaches for Michael's hand, much to his brother's surprise, but he takes it.

"HE'S YOURS!" Ambrose shouts, then he flings Michael towards Deprivation. The momentum makes him fly much harder and faster than usual. Michael gives Deprivation a tremendous kick to his stomach, winding him.

"And one more for the road!" Michael says, then he locks his hand together and pile drives his fists into Deprivation so hard that he leaves the Horseman lying in a crater.

"Why you worthless pieces of…." Deprivation shouts as he tries to get up, but then something pierces him in the back.

"ARGHHHHH!"

"What was that?" Ambrose taunts him as he approaches the crater where Deprivation is impaled by his own spear. "I didn't quite catch that."

"You will pay for this, BOY!"

"Who's the weakling now?" Ambrose asks as he jumps into the crater and lands beside Michael.

"Took you long enough!" Ambrose tells him.

"I could say the same for you!" Michael replies, then he hears a familiar voice. "Everything all good down there?"

"All good here!" Michael assures Quinn, who had flown to them holding Hannah.

"Who's he?" Quinn asks upon seeing Ambrose's demon wings. "And can we trust him?"

"He's my brother," Michaels says with a long forgotten pride, "and yes, we can trust him."

"You feel better now, your Highness?" Ambrose teases Quinn.

"Yeah, but you don't have to be a dick about it."

"What was that?" Ambrose demands.

"Nothing!"

"Enjoy this while you can!" Deprivation threatens them.

"Oh, we are!" Michael says, then he grinds the spear that is still lodged in Deprivation, who cries out in agony. Michael stops, but he retains his grip on the spear in case Deprivation tried to escape. "Now you're going to answer a few questions."

"Yeah, starting with which one of your brothers did this to me!" Ambrose says. "I need to know!"

"What makes you think I'll tell you anything?" Deprivation snarls. Hannah quivers behind Quinn who asks her, "Are you okay?"

"Yes, I just don't like his voice," Hannah replies.

"WHICH OF YOUR BROTHERS DID THIS TO ME?" Ambrose shouts at Deprivation.

"HA-HA-HA-HA!"

"You think this is funny?" Ambrose retorts, then he turns the spear to cause Deprivation more pain.

"If you don't like what you have become then maybe you shouldn't have excepted the deal!"

"What deal?" Michael asks Ambrose, who was visibly shaken.

"No, that was a dream!" he protests.

"They all say that at first!" Deprivation replies. "I'll tell you something, only because it doesn't matter. I can already feel my brothers on the move! When a Horseman recruits a human, we leave a mark on them, like a cattle brand. Find it and you will know which of my brothers have your soul!"

"Which Horseman are you?" Ambrose asks.

"He's Famine," Michael told him.

"Deprivation is the name! But yes I have been known as FAMINE!"

"Why are you here?" Michael asks.

"Question time is over!"

"NO! Answer me!" Michael says as he twists the spear, but Deprivation simply laughs and taunts, "The pain is growing on me!"

"He's not going to tell us anything, Michael," Ambrose says.

"I heard him say something about a SEAL!" Hannah shouts from the top of the crater.

"SHUT YOUR MOUTH ANGEL!"

Ambrose struck Deprivation, shutting him up, then he said, "Go on, girl."

"Uh, it's hazy… I was in and out of consciousness. But I did overhear him saying something about a seal… or seals?"

"SHUT UP!"

"If he interrupts again, kill him," Michael tells his brother.

"With pleasure," Ambrose smiles.

"Think Hannah!" Michael urges her. "Was there anything else?"

"I'm sorry, I can't…wait, it must be seals plural, because the four Horsemen had to open them and regroup here later!"

"Mean anything to you?" Ambrose asks Michael.

"No, but I know someone who might know."

"You're too late!" Deprivation tells them, "Everything is already in motion!"

"Oh really?" Michael replies.

"I just got the all-clear!" Deprivation grins as he taps his ear.

"Are they listening?" Ambrose asks as he looks around.

"I had two missions here tonight," Deprivation explains with a deathly stare. "I was merely a pawn in this game. Pawns have important roles, like protecting the more important pieces on the board. Can you tell me what their other function is, Michael?"

"They sacrifice themselves to draw the important pieces out."

"PRECISELY!" Deprivation replies.

Michael recalled Constable Sacks warning him that they know where he lived. "Oh God, they're at my home!" he cries out.

Deprivation begins to taunt him with a sinister laugh and Michael gazes upon him with anger. He reaches for the spear gripping it tight with both hands, he then raises it high into the air.

"NOOOO! Not the spear" Deprivation yells out.

The spear emits a glow and buzzes as if reacting to Michael's touch, "Argh!" Michael yells as he plunges the spear into Deprivation's face; as he does so, the heavens seem to react, sending down a lightning bolt striking the spear. The electrical current surges throughout Deprivations entire body, causing it to jolt about. Soon its body gives out and black tainted blood begins to ooze from every orifice.. Deprivations blood is thick and gives off a very pungent smell to everyone; Michael wastes no time and he takes to the sky with haste.

"Hey, where are you going?" Ambrose yells.

"My place, this is not over" Michael cries out

Ambrose acts quickly and grabs hold of the spear and flies after his brother.

Hannah turns to Quinn and says "we should go after them, in case Michael needs help."

"Okay, hop on," Quinn says, offering his back for Hannah to sit on, then he flies after Michael, leaving the ruined city behind. The people behind the police barrier watch the angels fly off in a hurry, then Natalie and her news crew duck under the barrier.

"HEY!" a police officer yells at them, "Wait until the area has been cleared!"

They ignore him and so do the rest of the crowd who investigate the city cautiously. Some buildings were still intact, some beyond repair.

Natalie arrives at the top of the crater and sees the dead Horseman.

"They did it!" she whisper, then as more people approach the crater she cries aloud, "They did it!"

Everyone cheers and celebrates, then Natalie asks her cameraman, "Where's the camera?"

"It's back in the helicopter."

"Well, go get it, quickly! The world needs to know it's not ending!"

Chapter 30

GOD?

"MICHAEL, WAIT UP!" Ambrose yells at Michael, but he doesn't listen and keeps flying so fast that his brother struggles to keep up.

"Father Brian are you there?' Michael prays.

'Yes. Is it over?'

"I don't know. I'm heading home and should be there shortly, but I'd appreciate it if you would check on my family. Would you do me this favour?"

'Yes, of course.'

"Thank you, Father!"

"Hey, brother, what's going on?" Ambrose asks as he catches up with Michael.

"I think my family may be in danger!" he replies as they approached his suburb.

"Look, they're descending!" Hannah says, pointing ahead while clinging to Quinn.

"Finally!" he gasps, exhausted.

Rather than glide down, Michael retracts his wings and lands heavily at the front of his house. "Kelly!" he shouts as he races inside. Ambrose lands and lodges the spear into the ground before following his brother.

"Kelly! Emma! Hudson! Isaiah!" Michael shouts as he searches the house, then Father Brian comes racing out from the lounge room.

"Michael, wait!" the priest says, placing a hand on the angel's bruised and bloodied chest.

"What's going on?" Michael asks as he tries to fight back tears. "Where is everyone?"

"I told the kids to find somewhere safe to hide," Father Brian explains, "but Michael…your wife—"

"DAD!" all the kids cry as they come racing out to hug Michael. He kneels and embraces them, then the boys yell out, "Uncle Ambrose!"

"Hey, Hudson… Isaiah," he says uncomfortably, for he has not seen his nephews in a while. "Emma." He gives her an awkward nod.

"Are you all okay?" Michael asks his children as Quinn and Hannah enter the room.

"Yes, but we had to hide," Hudson breaks off, upset, and looks around for his mother.

"He came from out of nowhere!" Father Brian begins to explain.

"Kel!" Michael says softly. He draws a deep breath, clenches his eyes shut and tries to find the courage to look into the lounge.

Quinn and Hannah look sorrowfully at each other, feeling Michael's pain.

"Kel!" Michael says as he finally steps into the lounge and sees his wife. Kelly is curled up in a ball on the couch, crying hysterically.

"Babe!" Kelly cries out as she rushes towards her husband and gives him a big hug.

"What happened?" Michael asks.

"He was terrifying!" Kelly replies, as she wipes tears from her face.

"Who was he?" Michael asks.

Kelly shrugs her shoulders, but Father Brian suggests, "I think he might be one of the other Horsemen."

"What did he want?" Michael asks Kelly. She looked down, unwilling to answer her husband. "What did he want, Kel?"

"He wanted a soul!" she replies reluctantly. "He seemed hell bent on one of the children's souls."

"WHAT!" Michael cringes as he speaks.

"I wouldn't let him," Kelly says in a stern manner. "I offered him my soul instead."

"You what!" Michael shouts, then his wife broke down in tears.

"Hun, I'm sorry," Michael says as he cradles his distressed wife in his arms.

"Michael, I tried," Father Brian says, "but for some reason he wouldn't take mine."

"It wants leverage, Father," Michael replies. "I'm just not sure what for."

"So, this isn't over?" Hannah asks. "I mean, how many more of those things are out there?"

"This is my good friend, Father Brian. He'll fill you all in on everything," Michael replies.

While Father Brian explains Apocalypse and the four Horsemen, Ambrose watches Michael and Kelly, who are having a private discussion.

"You okay, gorgeous?" Michael asks his wife.

"Yeah, I think so," she says as she brushes Isaiah's hair with her fingers as he clung tightly to her leg. "I feel the same, I just hate knowing that when I die, I'll be going somewhere that I didn't think existed," she sobs. "I won't be able to see any of my loved ones once I pass on."

"That's not going to happen, Hun!" Michael reassures her. "Cos I'm going to get your soul back."

"How?"

"I'll find a way."

"Find a way for what?" Ambrose asks as he approaches his brother and sister-in-law.

"I'm going to get my wife's soul back," Michael replies.

"You don't know how to do that!" Ambrose responds.

"True, I don't," Michael admits. "I was hoping you might know, Father."

"Me? No! I wouldn't know where to begin," Father Brian says. "I actually don't think it is possible."

"It is possible," a voice says. They all turned around to see a stranger through the front door. "I hope you don't mind, Michael, the door was open."

"YOU!" Michael groans.

"Michael, who is this?" Father Brian asks.

Michael's smile is wry. "This is God."

"WHAT!" Father Brian says in shock, then he falls to his knees and bows his head reverently.

"Should we kneel as well?" Quinn whispers to Hannah, who shrugs.

Ambrose looks at the new arrival with a touch of hatred as he comes closer to the group.

Michael wasn't pleased either. "We could've used your help earlier."

"Pfft! Don't expect any help from him!" Ambrose says with vitriol.

"Ooh, tension!" Quinn whispers to Hannah, who nudges him with an elbow to the ribs to silence him.

"Hey, have some respect!" Father Brian scolds Michael and Ambrose as he stands.

"That's okay, Father. They have their reasons to be upset with me."

"Well, can you get my wife's soul back?" Michael asks.

"I can't!"

"And why not?" Michael asks angrily.

"Because I am not God."

"What!" Michael says. "Well, who are you then?"

"I am the one that the dark forces fear," he says proudly. "I am the General of God's Army. I am—"

"Yeah, yeah, we get it," Ambrose interrupts. "You're the Archangel Michael."

"Hey! That is unacceptable!" Father Brian shouts. "I am sorry for his rudeness."

"Why did you impersonate God?" Michael asks the Archangel.

"I didn't. I simply didn't correct you."

"Fair enough," Michael says nonchalantly, "So what do you want?".

"I'm here to help you."

"How?"

"Hell," the Archangel answers. "I know how to get you there."

"What! Really?" Michael asks. "Wait, why do you want to help?"

"Because it's the right thing to do," the Archangel replies.

"I don't believe that for a second!"

"What's to believe?" Father Brian asks. "He's an Angel, *the* Archangel. His job is to help."

"No! He has lied to us once and he is not about to stop now," Michael replies, gazing at the Archangel with a look of contempt. "I'm not going anywhere with you unless you start by telling us the truth. So why do you really want to help us?"

"I knew I chose you for a reason," the Archangel says with a smile. "You're just as stubborn as I am."

"I'm nothing like you!"

The Archangel laughs. "Who are you trying to convince? Me, or yourself?"

There's an awkward silence as Michael and the Archangel glare at one another.

"Okay, Okay," Father Brian says, positioning himself between them. "I think we all need to take a breather."

When Michael and the Archangel break eye contact and turn their backs, both Quinn and Hannah sigh in relief.

"You want to know everything, Michael?" the Archangel asks. "Then I'll show you."

"How?"

"Easy," the Archangel answers, then he raises his hand to Michael's temple and said, "Everything that I know, you will know."

"How is that possible?" Michael asked, ducking his head away from the Archangel's hand.

"I can link your mind with mine. You will see everything through my eyes from the past to present. You will know the whole truth, but..."

"But what?"

"In order for this to be successful, I must use my last essence as an Archangel," he says with a touch of sorrow in his voice, but a resoluteness in his eyes.

"What does that mean?" Michael asks.

"It means I won't be an Archangel anymore," he replies. "I used most of my essence making you an angel, Michael. After this I will be human."

"What? No!" Father Brian interjects. "We're not doing this! You have served our Lord well and will continue to do so. We can't lose a soldier like you, not when this battle has barely begun!"

"I'm with Father Brian!" Michael says. "There is still so much for you to teach me...us." He waves his hand towards Quinn, Hannah and Ambrose. "We can't win this war without you!"

"It's okay, I want to do this," the Archangel reassures the priest as he places a nurturing hand on his shoulder, then he looks at Michael and says, "This war is already lost if that is your attitude. All your life you have held back. You have held back your anger, your grief, your love and most importantly your strength." He unexpectedly claps his hands together, startling everyone in the room. He keeps his hands together as he continues, "do not hide your emotions anymore; use them and pool them together." He moves his hands about as if moulding something within his palms. "Let that be your weapon, for this is the power of an Archangel." He opened his right hand which emitted a light glow, then he raised it to Michael's temple and asks, "Are you ready?"

Lost for words, Michael takes a while to respond. He looks the Archangel in the eyes before answering, "I'm ready."

The Archangel touches his temple. The glow from his hand is absorbed by Michael who clenches his eyes tight and feels his body become tense.

Quinn and Hannah look at each other with concern.

"MICHAEL!" Ambrose yells out, but Father Brian grabs hold of him to ensure he doesn't interrupt the ritual.

Deep within his subconscious, Michael witnesses a chain of events in flashes, as if someone has hit the rewind button and he is trying his best to focus on each scene as it flashes by.

It's a memory from the Archangel Michael. He overhears a conversation between a gathering of Archangels.

"Father is not answering?"

Michael asks, "What do you mean 'not answering'?"

"We don't know," the Archangel Gabriel replied. "Metatron believes God went to Eden after Christ died."

"No, He couldn't!" Michael responded.

"What is it?" Gabriel asked.

"God is going to resurrect Christ!"

A blinding light blurs the memory. Flashes occur once again, only this time it was fast forwarding to a new memory. Everything comes to a halt. The Archangels Gabriel and Michael were arguing.

"NO! Leave the humans!" Gabriel yells at Michael. "They deserve whatever is coming!"

"Brother, this is a new Age of Humans; they are not like the last," Michael replies. "They are much kinder—"

"We don't care! We have all watched them kill each other over the most frivolous of things—"

"Brother, Please—" Michael tries to interject, but the Archangel Uriel chimes in.

"Michael, Gabriel is right. These humans are not worth saving. They are savages and portray worrying behaviours like that of Lucifer. We will not help them in this war!"

A blinding light blurs the memory which skips forward again. This memory is more recent; it was hours before Michael was struck down by the lightning that descended from the Heavens. The Archangel Michael is delivering a motivational speech, trying to encourage his brothers to do the right thing and follow him to Earth.

"My brothers, I cannot persuade you to come with me. Only know that I must do this. You have seen for yourselves that Lucifer is afoot. His minions have already gathered on Eden." He pauses and looks on the faces of his troops before continuing, "If we don't do something now Eden will be lost to the dark forces. Don't do it for me; do it for our Father!" Gabriel steps forward and nods at Michael. "I'm with you!"

Michael nods back at Gabriel.

"So am I!" Raphael said as he stepped forward. All of the rest agreed, except for Uriel.

Michael doesn't encourage Uriel or force him to join them. Instead, he patiently waits for an answer. Uriel stepped forward and asked, "Do we get to choose our own champions?"

"Yes!" Michael replied. "Those that are deserving of our power and share our qualities."

"Then I'm in!" Uriel responded. The two shared a smile before they all got into their positions and looked down on Eden. Soon Eden went dark, which then made it easier for the Archangels to locate their champions.

Raphael said, "I have located mine. I hope to see you all soon."

He jumped down, crossing the threshold between Heaven and Earth, then he merged into a lightning bolt and struck a human on Earth.

"Okay, one down," Michael said as the rest of them tried to locate their champions.

Michael waited until all the others had gone except for Uriel.

"Are you sure about your human, Michael?" Uriel asked.

"Yes, I am certain of it. And you?"

"Oh yes, I have found mine. I think you will like my choice, and so will your champion!" Uriel said with a smile, then he lunged out of the heavens and into Earth's realm.

The Archangel Michael takes a quick glance down from the Heavens at the human he has chosen.

"Hannah," Michael whispered.

"Michael," she replied.

"What!" the Archangel was surprised that Michael was able to speak during the link up of their two minds. He made his memory skip forwards once again. *The Archangel is peering down on Michael's smoking crisp body while the ambulance officers work diligently to revive him. They zap his body with the defibrillator but to no avail.*

"No! This can't be!" the Archangel cried out. "No, please!"

"Okay, one last time," the ambulance officer echoed in the memory which was slowed down. As the ambulance officers counted down, the Archangel placed a hand on Michael's chest and looking up at the heavens pleading, "Please, don't take this soul just yet. He is destined for more!"

The last zap from the defibrillator jolted Michael's body. The Archangel kept his hand on his chest praying as the defibrillator explodes sending both ambulance officers flying.

There is still no movement from Michael's body. Whilst everyone was regaining their composure, the Archangel knelt and whispered to Michael, "Get up! A war is coming; the world needs you more than ever. I have put all my faith into you. Please, you can't die now!" The Archangel begins to cry over Michael's body and makes a last plea, "Your family needs you."

'BEEP!'

This harmonious noise brought joy to the Archangel who smiled. As the second heartbeat was heard, Michael woke from the mind link up with his Archangel.

"You were there the whole time," Michael says sorrowfully, feeling guilty for having misjudged the Archangel Michael.

"You were my responsibility; I couldn't leave you!"

"Okay, what just happened?" Ambrose asks.

Michael was still coming to his senses from the ordeal, so Ambrose asked again, "Well? What happened?"

"I saw everything!" Michael tells his brother, then he looks at Quinn, Hannah and Father Brian and says with much regret "There is a war coming, and God is missing."

"So where does that leave us?" Quinn asks.

"It means we're on our own."

"NO!" the archangel responds as he stands in front of the group. "We still have one option. In fact, it's our only option!"

"And what's that?" Michael asks.

"Hell. We must go there."

Michael looks at the Archangel curiously and says, "I know why I want to go there, but tell me why you want to go there?"

"I believe our Father is held prisoner there."

"WHAT!" Father Brian exclaims. The others all express their concerns as well.

"How do you know this?" Michael asks. "I didn't see anything that alluded to this in your memories."

"It's a. . ." The Archangel has some trouble finding the right words. "What you humans would call a 'gut feeling'. I have searched everywhere for Him. It only makes sense that the one place I didn't look may yet have Him."

Everyone in the room looks at one other while silently contemplating the game plan that would involve rescuing God from Hell.

"Think about it: why else is there so much evil in the world?" the Archangel continues sadly. "Our Father is not here to strike down the evil that now plagues this world. Please, I can't do this alone. Help me save our Father."

Michael walks over to the Archangel and holds out his hand. "I will help you, but my wife comes first."

The Archangel Michael grins from ear to ear and shakes Michael's hand. "Thank you."

Michael exchanges a worried look with Ambrose. They both know that the journey ahead will be a dangerous one, for no human had ever travelled to Perdition and back. Mind you, neither of them was completely human anymore, which gave them an advantage. "So, how do we get to Hell?" Michael asks the Archangel.

Acknowledgements

Writing this book has been a journey I could not have taken alone.

I want to extend my heartfelt gratitude to my first editor, **Charmaine Cave**, for your invaluable guidance and belief in this story from the very beginning. Your insight helped me shape these pages into something I am proud to share.

To my second editor, **Nina Peck**, thank you for your sharp eye, thoughtful suggestions, and care in polishing this manuscript. Your expertise has made this book shine.

To my family and friends, your unwavering support and patience kept me grounded and motivated when doubt crept in.

Finally, to the readers — your time and imagination are the greatest gifts a new author could ask for. Thank you for embarking on this journey with me.

About the Author

A devoted family man, Michael Dann is married with three children and treasures the time he spends with them above all else. His journey into writing began unexpectedly with Save the Dreamtime, a children's story inspired by Aboriginal culture and mythology. The book weaves themes of family, heritage, and adventure, reflecting his deep appreciation for the power of storytelling.

With a background in Business Management (Edith Cowan University) and Business Law (Murdoch University), Michael never set out to be an author, yet completing his first book revealed a truth he couldn't ignore, some stories demand to be told.

That realization gave rise to *The Fall of Eden*, his first full-length fantasy novel and the opening volume in an epic trilogy. A story idea first imagined in his teenage years, it has since evolved into a sweeping tale of sacrifice, destiny, and the eternal struggle between light and darkness. The second book in the series is already in development.

With his writing, he has gained a newfound respect for the dedication authors bring to balancing creativity with everyday life. For him, family remains the heart of all things, even as he continues to explore new worlds through the written word.

254